Dear Romance Reader,

Welcome to a world of breathtaking passion and never-ending romance.

Welcome to *Precious Gem Romances*.

It is our pleasure to present *Precious Gem Romances,* a wonderful new line of romance books by some of America's best-loved authors. Let these thrilling historical and contemporary romances sweep you away to far-off times and places in stories that will dazzle your senses and melt your heart.

Sparkling with joy, laughter, and love, each *Precious Gem Romance* glows with all the passion and excitement you expect from the very best in romance. Offered at a great affordable price, these books are an irresistible value—and an essential addition to your romance collection. Tender love stories you will want to read again and again, *Precious Gem Romances* are books you will treasure forever.

Look for eight fabulous new *Precious Gem Romances* each month—available only at Wal★Mart.

Lynn Brown, Publisher

D1354014

A MILLION TOMORROWS

Marylee Anderson

ZEBRA BOOKS
KENSINGTON PUBLISHING CORP.

Thanks to the unwavering support of Carolyn, Ellen, Leanne, Peggy, and the Virginia Romance Writers.

ZEBRA BOOKS are published by

Kensington Publishing Corp.
850 Third Avenue
New York, NY 10022

Copyright © 1996 by Marylee Anderson

All rights reserved. No part of this book may be reproduced in any form or by any means without the prior written consent of the Publisher, excepting brief quotes used in reviews.

If you purchased this book without a cover you should be aware that this book is stolen property. It was reported as "unsold and destroyed" to the Publisher and neither the Author nor the Publisher has received any payment for this "stripped book."

Zebra and the Z logo Reg. U.S. Pat. & TM Off.

First Zebra Printing: July, 1996
10 9 8 7 6 5 4 3 2 1

Printed in the United States of America

SUBMARINE SATELLITE
INFORMATION EXCHANGE

COMMANDER MARK J. EDWARDS, USN
USS *SILVERSHIP*
MARK:
RETURNING HOME TO BOSTON, I REALIZED COMMON
SENSE TEMPORARILY DESERTED ME STOP I'M SURE YOU
UNDERSTAND WHY I MUST WITHDRAW MY ACCEP-
TANCE OF YOUR MARRIAGE PROPOSAL STOP THANKS
FOR MAKING MY THANKSGIVING CRUISE ONE I'LL AL-
WAYS REMEMBER STOP WISHING YOU THE BEST LIFE
OFFERS STOP

—Cecilia Hargrave Mason

One

It's my own fault. Celie Mason scolded herself as she negotiated the slick steps to her restored brownstone. Apparently she was the only one who'd presumed the springlike balm bathing Boston the previous two days would last through the weekend. Tonight everyone she had passed was properly bundled in winter coats and boots, fully prepared for the snowstorm that blanketed the city during rush hour.

Her toes throbbed a vicious protest as she stamped loose the sleet caked to her shoes. She'd trade her family fortune for a cup of hot tea the moment she stepped into the house. Wishful thinking; at noon she'd watched Shannon, her housemate, board a jet to Nassau. Tonight the house would be empty.

Shivering, Celie punched the security code into the electronic lock securing her front door. Once inside the foyer, her relief at the welcoming wall of warmth vanished when she heard the unmistakable rush of water through the pipes.

"Not again," she muttered, dropping her briefcase and kicking off her wet shoes. She hurried to the laundry room. After digging out a wrench from the toolbox, she forced the master water valve counterclockwise until the gushing faded to a trickle.

So much for tea. A burst pipe two weeks earlier had proved firsthand the improbability of locating a plumber on a Friday night.

Think like an optimist, she told herself. With Christmas just around the corner, maybe she could bribe someone to work for triple the standard fee. Maybe this time the water damage to the swirled plaster walls and ceilings would be minimal. And maybe there really was a Santa Claus.

In the living room, Celie switched on a lamp, then peeled off her sodden raincoat. She glanced up when a board creaked overhead. "Shannon?" she called, too late remembering no one else should be in the house.

Over the pulse hammering in her ears, she listened to the foot-steps above as she tried to decide whether to run or hide.

Panic kept her rooted in one spot. Unable to do anything else, she prayed the intruder wasn't carrying a gun.

As in a horror movie, time seemed to slow to a crawl. Not daring to breathe, she watched one bare foot and then another come into view, followed by muscular legs, her own yellow bath towel, a well-muscled chest, and finally a face.

Mark Edwards. Recognition leached away her fear replacing it with a more unsettling response. He seemed taller than she remembered, although some logical section of her brain pointed out that that made sense, since she now stood before him shoeless. What she couldn't explain was her reaction to him, which seemed just as potent now as it had been the first time they'd met.

He paused at the landing to wipe a second towel over his military-short black hair. "Forget to pay the water bill, Celie?"

Ignoring the surge of sensation swamping her, she tried to pull herself together. She'd already lost her head over him once and had spent the last three weeks attempting to recover. She prided herself on never making the same mistake twice, no matter how tempting that mistake might be.

She'd also been reared to remain cool and collected, no matter what the circumstance, but despite her up bringing, her mind went numb. Unable to focus on any of the dozen questions swirling through her head, she answered inanely, "I turned off the master valve."

Her heart pounded double-time at his smile. Regardless of her determination not to recall them, memories of the week they had shared flooded her mind.

Failing miserably at maintaining her composure, she concentrated on something less disturbing than the man who stood so close he seemed to block out the rest of the room. She frowned at the rug underneath his bare feet. "You're dripping on my Aubusson."

Grinning, he stepped back onto the bottom step and slung the towel around his neck. "Sorry."

She tried to organize the questions crowding her mind, but while she groped for one to ask first, her resolve to keep her gaze trained on his face failed miserably.

She couldn't help notice his shoulders bore traces of the tan he'd acquired during the Thanksgiving cruise where they'd met. Her glance bounced over his muscled stomach and to the towel's edge before she caught herself and jerked her attention back to his face. His gold-flecked blue eyes glinted as if he could read every confused thought tumbling through her head.

Years ago she had perfected the art of concealing her emotions, come hell or high water. But Mark Edwards's appearance proved more disrupting than either.

Certainly he had a logical explanation for surfacing uninvited in her living room. Once she knew what it was, she'd be better able to assess and then handle the situation.

When it didn't appear he intended to volunteer any information, she asked point-blank, "What are you doing here?"

"Looking at you. You look great."

She could just imagine. Aware that the wind had torn apart her French braid, she lifted a hand to smooth her tangled hair. Catching herself mid-action, she instead pushed away a strand clinging to her cheek, telling herself what Mark thought or how she looked had nothing to do with the issue at hand.

Conscious of his gaze sliding over her, she fought an urge to smooth her water-stained emerald silk skirt. He was trespassing, and if she had any sense she'd throw him out, bare chest and all, into the dark winter night.

Then again, she reminded herself, if she had any sense at all, he wouldn't be standing in her living room. She never would have boarded the cruise ship three weeks ago, never would have spoken to him in the dawn's early light, never would have lost her head, never would have made a foolish promise to marry him.

As if he could read her mind, he smiled. It took every ounce of her self-control to keep from returning it, to keep from recalling the week of breakfasts, lunches, dinners, and all the pleasure-filled moments in between they'd shared.

Cursing her ability to recall even the smallest details, she repeated her question. "What are you doing here?"

"In Boston?"

If he hadn't flashed that self-assured smile she'd swear he was playing for time. For the moment she decided to go along with his game, whatever it was. "In my home. In my bathroom." *In my life.*

"Shannon let me in this morning, told me to help myself to the fridge, television, whatever. She forgot to mention you were having problems with the plumbing."

Realizing she should have suspected her matchmaking friend from the start, Celie bit back a sigh. "I saw her at the airport a few hours ago. I guess she *forgot* to mention she'd left you behind. And we aren't having problems. A pipe burst a few weeks ago, so when I came home and heard the water running, I figured it had happened again. I'm sorry. It never occurred to me to check the bathroom first."

She couldn't believe she heard herself apologizing. After all, he'd invaded *her* home.

He didn't give her time to inform him of that fact. "Shannon said you never get home before six o'clock. I thought I'd be showered and dressed for dinner when you arrived."

His smile tempted her to apologize again. If he'd been squat and bald and potbellied, she'd be better able to deal with the situation. The longer she looked at him, the harder she found it to focus on what she should say. Was there, she wondered, a gracious way to invite someone *out* of your home? None came to mind, and she heard herself again explaining to him instead of vice versa. "The Resource Center closed early because of the weather."

He walked toward her, and not knowing what else to do, she heard herself babbling about the predicted blizzard, about how she'd missed hearing the forecast, how she'd slogged the two miles home from work through sleet and snow.

Still smiling, he took the coat she clutched to her chest and dropped it onto the floor. He pulled the towel from around his neck free and used it to blot dry her hair.

Proximity played havoc with her senses. She could smell her soap on his skin. She felt his breath flutter against her cheek when he wrapped the towel around her shoulders and tugged the ends to draw her closer until only inches separated them.

Although it had been three weeks since she'd kissed him, she could still remember the way his mouth tasted, recall the feel of his lips on hers. That memory made her lift her head even as her mind roared a warning to shove him away.

Things were getting out of hand, just as they had done aboard ship. Only she wasn't on a singles' cruise now; she was back home in Boston.

"Mark, wait—"

She flattened her palms against his chest, but before she could push him away, he'd captured her hands in his. "I have waited," he whispered. "Three long weeks. Twenty-one miserable days. Five-hundred-plus lonely hours."

She knew she should resist, knew he'd release her at once if she did, but the intensity of his gaze made her forget to do the proper thing. Seemingly on its own accord, her chilled skin surged against the warmth of his.

"I missed you," he said, his voice a caress that coaxed her even closer. Pushing her jacket from her shoulders, he let it tumble to the floor while he turned his attention to the seed-pearl buttons securing her ivory blouse. "You'll catch pneumonia if you don't get out of these wet clothes."

There was something she ought to say to send him away, but nothing came to mind as heat from his fingers flowed through the dampened silk. In the hollow of his neck she could see his pulse beating as fast as her own. His lips skimmed over her hair, and she knew if she lifted her head another inch he would kiss her. And she'd kiss him back.

Then she'd be hopelessly lost, overcome by the same emotional tempest that had landed her in this situation in the first place, a situation she thought, until he walked down her stairs, she now had well under control.

He brushed his fingers over her collarbone. "Goose bumps. You're shivering."

She was, not from the cold, but from an aching awareness that kept her from doing the sensible thing and distancing herself, physically and emotionally. Just one minute more, she promised herself, savoring the rise and fall of his chest against her cheek, the thudding of his heart against her hands.

Her blouse finally unbuttoned, he pulled it free and tossed it aside, then wrapped the towel shawl-like around her shoulders. "Go put on something warm and dry."

A very sensible suggestion, one she should have thought of instead of losing herself in his arms. Which, she realized as she stepped back, was exactly what she'd almost done.

Determined to regain the upper hand, she clutched the towel and once again sought an answer to her question. "You still haven't explained why you're here."

"It's Christmas."

"Nearly Christmas." She scooped up her blouse and jacket. "You told me your tour wouldn't end until spring."

"We docked this morning for emergency repairs."

She pulled the edges of the towel closer together when she realized he seemed fascinated by the lacy edge of her bra. "Which still doesn't explain—"

"I'm finding it impossible to talk shop when you're standing half-dressed within reach."

The invitation behind his words and slow smile made her feel fevered, too much so to attribute to her home's efficient central heating system. Excusing herself, she hurried upstairs before she could do something imprudent.

In the mirror in her bedroom, as she yanked her hair into its customary French braid, she noticed the sleet had washed away her makeup. Her pale skin must have been blue-tinged earlier when she came inside, although now slashes of color swept over her cheeks.

She hadn't blushed in years. Annoyance, she decided, or apprehension. Maybe a combination of both. He'd caught her off guard, as any man walking half-naked down her steps would. Then again, he would have caught her off guard had he appeared in camouflage fatigues.

She heard him go into the bathroom and close the door. Her pulse and wits should have returned to normal by now, since she was no longer threatened by an intruder. Yet she still felt off balance, not at all ready to confront Mark again.

Maybe she should have dialed 911 and pretended, when the police arrived, that she didn't know Mark. Immediately she dismissed that idea as the most cowardly solution she could imagine. Besides, he probably would have waved the lettergram she'd sent as irrefutable evidence she had lied, the police would have written off the call as a domestic disturbance, and she'd still have Mark on her hands.

To borrow her grandmother's favorite expression, instead of jumping the fence, she needed to take the bull by the horns.

She'd go downstairs and have a cup of tea. Then, her sanity restored, she'd handle this like a meeting of good friends who'd once shared something special but were now content to live with the memories—memories she refused at the moment to think about, knowing there'd be time for that later.

There was a reason he'd dropped into Boston, and once she found out what it was, she could settle things in a manner satisfactory to them both.

A few minutes later, dressed in red wool slacks and a matching sweater, she ran down the stairs, stopping on her way to open the main water valve before she went into the kitchen. After switching on the radio, she filled a cup with water and placed it in the microwave to heat, then stared out the window at the snow whipping through the night.

Wearing an unlined raincoat and open-toed shoes, she'd just plunged through a blizzard and survived. Certainly she had the stamina to handle an uninvited guest and treat him with the courtesy he deserved while escorting him out the door.

"It's real pretty."

She jumped at Mark's soft words and spun around, almost colliding with him. With an interest she didn't want to have, she noticed how his tailored Navy dress blues emphasized his athletic frame. He'd played football at Annapolis, he'd told her, and she doubted he'd gained an ounce since then. Only the fine web of character lines at the corner of his eyes revealed he was nearing forty.

Conscious that the unsettling awareness she thought she'd tamped down was flowering again, she leaped into the role of perfect hostess. "May I offer you a cup of tea?"

"Coffee, if you have it."

Grateful for the distraction, she busied herself making a mug of instant coffee before she filled a tea ball and steeped it in her own cup of steaming water. Carrying both drinks to the kitchen table, she motioned for him to sit.

She offered him cream and sugar and watched him add too much of both to his coffee. Slipping into a chair across from him, she stirred her tea and waited for him to talk. Now that they were behaving like rational adults, she'd find out why he came and what he wanted.

Aboard ship he hadn't known her family owned more of New England than seemed legally possible. What he'd learned in the past weeks, especially since she'd signed her middle name—Hargrave—to the lettergram, she couldn't tell. He didn't seem the type to demand a payoff in exchange for disappearing into the woodwork, but then, she'd been fooled before.

She wished she didn't have to be so suspicious. Aboard ship she thought he'd been different from all the rest. Now, much as it hurt to think otherwise, she just wasn't sure. She decided to proceed cautiously with her questions.

While she debated how to approach the subject, he spoke. "I'm taking you to dinner."

Uneasy, she returned her cup to its saucer. How could he pretend things were the same? Had someone agreed to marry her, then reneged via a satellite lettergram, she'd be spitting mad and demanding an explanation.

"Shannon suggested a place." He pulled his wallet from his trouser pocket, withdrew a slip of paper, and read it aloud. "The Upper Crust."

Her roommate *would* choose the most romantic restaurant in the city, probably the only one on the continent that still employed a strolling violinist. It was an intimate hideaway for lovers, not at all intended for two people who'd met, shared a few magic moments, and were now saying good-bye.

At least, *she'd* said good-bye.

Perhaps her lettergram had been too vague. She needed to make certain now that he understood things were over, that she'd simply been swept off her feet and had allowed her heart to speak before her mind had had a chance to consider and reject his proposal.

It certainly had been easier writing a farewell speech on a blank sheet of paper. Unable to think of a tactful preamble, she decided to tackle the topic head-on. "You shouldn't have come."

"Why not?"

Expecting a full-fledged argument, she could only stare at him. She'd made it painfully clear when she had written the lettergram, taking care when selecting the limited number of words allowed so Mark would understand without a doubt that they had no future together.

"I've spent so many holidays aboard ships and subs I've lost count," he said. "When the sub limped back to port this morning, it seemed like a wish come true, being able to share our first Christmas together."

She should have realized anyone with enough ambition to scale the military corporate ladder so quickly wouldn't be easily dissuaded. Swallowing back the panic fluttering in her throat, she strove for a matter-of-fact tone. "I—we won't be sharing anything. I explained it in my lettergram."

"What did you explain?"

So he was going to drag her over the coals and make her admit she'd been impulsive. He would demand an apology and probably a little something extra to soothe his wounded ego.

She knew he deserved the apology. "About us," she said. "About me, I mean. About the mistake I made when I agreed to marry you."

She paused, offering him an opportunity to object, to argue, to tell her how much she'd hurt him.

Instead, he sat and watched her, letting several silent moments pass until she felt compelled to speak again. "I had a wonderful time, but that's expected on a pleasure cruise. We had no business considering marriage, let alone thinking we'd fallen in love in a week. People just don't fall in love at first sight."

He drank his coffee, studying her over the rim of the mug before he spoke. "Speak for yourself."

Her heart sank as she sensed his stubborn refusal to yield. "I think I can speak for us both," she said. "Infatuation fades, and we have nothing else but that in common."

"I love you."

"You don't . . . I don't . . ." Why couldn't she speak elegantly and succinctly instead of stuttering like a tongue-tied child? She forced herself to sip her tea, giving her common sense a chance to recoup before she tried again to explain. "We only shared a week, Mark. You don't really know me.

"I love you."

Her throat tightened, making a reply impossible. She refused to even consider his words. Love at first sight didn't exist, at least not in her life.

"Do you have a cold heart, Celie?" he drawled. "Or cold feet?"

Here she was trying to detail a rational decision, and he was talking hearts and flowers. She managed a smile but couldn't meet his direct gaze. "Neither. What we had was nice, but it's over. I'm sorry you traveled all this way. You should have called first."

"I did, this morning. You'd already left for work, so Shannon said she'd tell you—"

"She didn't."

"And she thought it wonderful that I'd travel so far to spend Christmas with my fiancée."

"Ex-fiancée," Celie corrected, a bit too quickly.

Knowing the deep breath he drew would most likely be a prelude to an argument, she rushed to thwart it before it started. "My agreement to marry you was impulsive. Too much moonlight, too much wine . . . I'm sorry, I really am. I sent the lettergram the day after you sailed so you could pursue other interests."

Wincing at her choice of words, she held her breath and waited for his inevitable outburst. She'd encountered wounded male pride often enough to expect one, although the last thing she ever intended to do was hurt him. She saw no reason he should suffer for her rash decision.

"You sent me a Dear John letter?"

She blinked at the amused disbelief coloring his words, the possibility that he hadn't received her note flooring her for a few sec-

onds. While that would justify his surprise arrival and lack of out-
rage, it also meant he had come to Boston because he wanted to,
not because he planned to seek compensation the way some other
men in her past had. Although it really shouldn't matter, the fact
he hadn't come in search of a payoff pleased her so much she had
to bite the inside of her cheek to keep a relieved smile at bay.

"I wrote to tell you we had no future." Since she'd intended on
presenting her reasoning in a businesslike manner, she was startled
to hear that her voice sounded gentle, almost wistful. She cleared
her throat. "I've had plenty of time to think things over the past
few weeks. We're just not right for each other. I know you'll find
someone else."

Her smile tightened just saying the last words, but she'd long
ago learned to isolate her feelings from decisions that had to be
made. "Someone more suitable," she added when he said nothing.

Mark swirled the last inch of coffee in his cup. "Have you found
someone else?"

It would be so easy to nod and simply end the discussion.
"There's no one else," she heard herself say before she had time
to give in to temptation.

"You couldn't have thought much about your decision if you
wrote me the day after I left."

She'd thought of nothing else for the past three weeks, but she
knew some things were better left unsaid.

"This is the first time I've ever regretted the lack of a pedigreed
background," he said.

His remark stung. How could he not understand her action had
been based on common sense, not her money or his lack of it. Seeing
the muscles in his jaw knot, she held her teacup in her hands to keep
from touching him and soothing the hurt she'd inflicted. "Neither
your background nor mine has anything to do with this."

"What does?"

If she'd expected the worst and anticipated his arrival, she'd have
memorized several solid reasons. Now she found herself groping
for just one. "The fact that two people can't build a marriage solely
based on sexual attraction."

"Sexual attraction." He repeated her words, drawing them out
as if that might help him understand. His frown said he didn't.
"Did the week we shared mean *anything* to you?"

Her kitchen seemed to grow smaller and warmer by the minute.
Whatever made her think this was an issue they could discuss po-

litely over a cup of tea? He was going to make her perform an emotional striptease.

Her grandmother would have told her to just shrug, wish him well, and send him on his way. But Celie knew she owed him the truth. While it would have been easier to stare into her teacup and speak, she forced herself to look into his dark-fringed eyes. "At the time it meant everything, but looking back, I see it must have been sheer infatuation, nothing else. I probably needed a change in my life, something different, and you were there . . ."

She stopped, because her words sounded lame. How could he understand that when she stepped onto the cruise ship she'd flung caution to the wind, and that it had returned full force the moment she'd boarded a plane back to Boston?

"Great fun, but just one of those things?"

She winced, although the song verse he paraphrased summed it up better at the moment than she could. "Something like that."

"And without giving it a chance, you're certain our marriage would fail."

Not knowing what else to say, she relied on an old standby. "Call it woman's intuition, if you must."

Tension bunched the muscles in her shoulders. If he demanded more reasons, she had none to give. Despite what he must think, it hadn't been a decision she'd made painlessly or irrationally. Aboard ship, she'd listened to her heart. In the real world, her mind ruled.

When he said nothing, she extended her hand, hating the awkwardness of the gesture but determined to keep their parting impersonal. "I wish you well, Mark."

He looked at her hand, then shook his head. "I can think of better ways to say farewell."

The conversation was definitely finished. Avoiding both the unspoken questions and the hurt in his eyes, she stood, gathered the cups, and carried them to the sink.

He followed. Watching her rinse the cups, he waited until she'd turned off the water to speak. "I realize I've made a nuisance of myself. Let me buy you dinner; it's the least I can do."

She saw a chance to retreat with her dignity intact. Appreciating his gesture, she smiled as she dried her hands on a linen towel, this time thinking before she spoke. "Mark, I'm the one who owes you an apology. It never occurred to me you hadn't received the letter-gram."

He shrugged. "You haven't said yes to dinner. No strings at-

tached, I promise. Well, one string—I don't have a car, so maybe
you could drop me at the airport after we eat."

Surprised at her deflated feeling, she nodded. He was leaving,
no strings attached—exactly the words she wanted to hear, yet a
part of her wished he hadn't surrendered so willingly. If she'd sub-
consciously harbored a yearning that they really were meant to be
together, his statement certainly quelled it.

After all, did she really need someone who insisted he loved her
one minute and made plans to fly out of her life the next? Then
again, what more should she expect from a man who had wooed
five fiancées but had married none? She'd laughed about it when
he'd confessed aboard ship, but wondered now whether there was
truth in the cliché "Easy come, easy go."

"Dinner, yes; the Upper Crust, no." As she walked into the living
room, she considered an alternative restaurant, something more
accommodating for tourists than lovers. "Let's eat at the Bay Tower
Room. You'll get a great view of Boston with your dinner."

"Sounds good." He pulled on his overcoat. "Give me the keys;
I'll warm your car. Which one is it?"

"Blue Subaru, although it's probably white at the moment. I
didn't drive today, so it's covered with snow. There's a brush and
a scraper on the passenger-side floor."

Outside, Mark stopped for a few seconds to stare at the street
carpeted with snow.

So far, so good. He'd taken a gamble by showing up even though
he'd received the lettergram telling him in no uncertain terms what
they had was over.

His gut feeling told him she considered the week they'd shared
aboard the ship more than just a fling. She'd been as dazed as he,
their lives both altered by a true meeting of souls. He'd been prudent
enough to realize it; now he needed to convince her of the same.

On his way to Boston, he'd vowed not to touch her until he'd
convinced her there was something much deeper, something more
profound than sexual attraction pulling them together. Now, not
only had his resolve shattered the moment she walked back into
his life, but he was finding it harder by the minute to pretend he
wasn't at all affected by her panicked decision to back out the
moment his boat set sail.

First, he reminded himself stoically, he needed to strip away the
layers of reserve she'd built to conceal her feelings. Probably some
Calvinistic-tinted genetic guilt nagged her conscience for falling

in love so quickly. While they had much to learn about each other, he had no doubt they'd already formed that intangible bond vital to true love and marriage.

After he persuaded her to admit the same over dinner, he'd pull the lettergram out of his pocket so they could share a laugh over her premarital jitters. Then they'd make plans to live happily ever after.

A vicious gust of wind jolted him back to reality and a bitterly cold night in Boston. First things first, he told himself, and started poking through the snow-covered mounds along the curb until he located a blue Subaru.

Two

After getting her boots from the hall closet, Celie sat on the sofa to pull them on. It took considerable willpower not to look up a few moments later when Mark pushed open the foyer door, but she knew if he treated her to his smile once more, she might find herself changing her mind and inviting him to stay.

Seeing him board the first plane to Florida seemed the most sensible solution, one she was determined to carry through. She heard him rub his hands together, whether from the cold or from impatience, she couldn't tell when she'd finally steeled herself enough to look up. She caught a curiously guarded expression on his face.

"Be ready in a minute," she said, praying the evening wouldn't prove too difficult. She'd have no trouble keeping his mind occupied with thoughts other than their broken engagement. When prompted, people loved talking about themselves. There were a thousand questions she could ask regarding his extensive travels. In no time, dinner would be finished, and Mark would be at the airport.

In an hour or two, she'd be home again. Alone.

Unaccustomed to the wave of disappointment washing over her, she forced herself to think about the files she'd earlier stuffed into her briefcase. She'd brought home more than enough work to keep her mind occupied, to forget him and the week they had shared.

The thought should have appeased her; instead, it made her jerk the metal zipper to her boot into place with an impatience she seldom exhibited.

Both boots on, she stood. His lingering half smile made her uneasy. Although things were progressing smoothly, she didn't trust fate enough to think she was home free. She'd try to treat Mark like one of the polite acquaintances she occasionally dated, keeping him at arm's length, so to speak, even though he'd managed to get closer to her in a week than anyone else ever had. She found that thought unsettling. The sooner this evening ended, she decided, the better.

"Your door locks are frozen shut," he told her. "Maybe we should call out for a pizza."

She immediately dismissed that idea. In a restaurant it would be easier to pretend they were nothing more than casual friends sharing dinner. She silently selected topics to cover—weather, politics, sports—as she slipped on her ski jacket and found a can of de-icer in the hall closet.

Outside, the cutting wind sucked away her breath. Closing her eyes for a moment against the needling shafts of sleet, she fumbled for her hood and pulled it around her face. She gripped the railing to steady herself while she descended the slick steps, walking in the footprints he'd made minutes earlier.

The street appeared deserted, its scattered drifts of snow yet undisturbed by tire tracks. She pushed through the wind, shaking her head as she neared her car. With the illumination from the street-lamps, she could see a sheen of ice beneath the snow Mark had brushed away.

He pulled the can of de-icer from her hands and anchored it into the snow cloaking the car's hood. "Come on," he said, grabbing her hand. "There's a little diner down the street. I ate lunch there."

Not Vera's. Knowing if they went there they were bound to get the third degree, Celie grabbed his sleeve. "Let's go back inside and call for a pizza," she said, repeating his earlier suggestion.

Her voice vanished in a brutal gust of wind. It seemed useless to argue; his mind obviously made up, he wrapped his arm around her waist and headed down the street.

When he pushed open the curtained glass door of the diner, a string of brass sleigh bells jingled, announcing their arrival. Even as Celie hoped they'd be lost in the dinner rush, she saw they were the only customers in the cozy restaurant.

The gray-haired owner hurried toward them. "I was beginning to think you weren't coming in tonight," she said to Celie. "Sent my waitresses home, business being so slow. Hang your coats up there on the rack; it's plenty warm in here."

She arched her eyebrows as she inspected Mark. "Seen you in here this afternoon, didn't I? You don't look like one of her clients."

Mark grinned. "I'm her—"

"Friend," Celie interjected, hastily finishing his sentence. "Vera, Commander Mark Edwards. He's on his way back to Florida."

Mark held Celie's chair until she sat, then he slipped into the one next to hers. He shook his head when Vera offered him a hand-printed menu. "I don't know much about Boston fare. Bring me whatever you think's best."

Vera beamed. "Big bowl of chicken-and-barley stew's what you need today. How about you, dear?"

"Just hot tea and a salad, please," Celie said. "I'm not very hungry." Such a simple meal would assure they'd be finished eating in record time, before Vera's curiosity got the best of her.

"On a cold night like this?" Vera clucked her tongue. "A body needs more than that. Look at you wastin' away, so thin it's pitiful. What you need"—she stared pointedly at Mark—"is someone to take care of you."

Celie had heard the same line from Vera before. This time, however, it took her longer to manage a smile. "I appreciate your concern, but really, I'm doing just fine by myself."

Vera sniffed. "Comin' home at midnight, some days. Next morning, you're in here at dawn for breakfast."

"You work the same hours," Celie pointed out, a smile softening her words, "or you wouldn't see me."

"True, true, but I run this place. Besides, who'd look after you if I didn't?" Vera bustled away from the table.

Celie unfolded her red-and-white-checked napkin and tried to think of a harmless opening topic.

Mark didn't give her a chance. "So you eat here often?"

"Often enough that Vera thinks she needs to take me under her wing."

Mark glanced at the pass-through window and watched Vera work. "She reminds me of my mother," he said after a moment.

Celie fished through the basket of cellophane-wrapped crackers in the middle of the table. She knew Mark was a career officer soon to retire; that was more than enough background. Learning about his family might make it harder to say good-bye.

Instead of quelling the subject, her silence seemed to encourage him to continue. "Spends all her spare time in the kitchen. Sends me a box of cookies every week when I'm ashore—peanut-butter chocolate chip."

Determined as she was to keep personal observations to a minimum, Celie couldn't help envying him. Still, she tried not to invite any other information, murmuring, "That's nice."

"Beats lettergrams any day."

She felt her cheeks heat at his seemingly innocent remark. She refused to consider whether he mentioned that to make her feel guilty. It did. "It wasn't as if I could pick up the phone and call you," she pointed out.

Her words sounded more defensive than she intended, so she smiled to show she knew where the blame belonged—solely in her own hands. "Since you weren't due back in port until spring, it seemed cruel to let you think I'd be there when you returned."

"Maybe you were afraid I'd try to talk you out of changing your mind."

Shannon had argued herself hoarse urging her to wait, to reconsider. Much as Celie hated to admit it, her roommate had been right about one thing—sending the lettergram hadn't made her feel any better. She still caught herself thinking about Mark at the most inopportune times. Morning, noon, and night.

"You couldn't talk me into changing my mind," she said, knowing it wasn't totally true. The fact that he probably could made it even more important to send him on his way as soon as possible. Otherwise, they'd share a few more enchanted days, then the moment his plane took off and her feet were back on the ground, she'd be twice as miserable as she'd been the first time she'd waved good-bye.

He smiled suddenly, his eyes warm, and she felt the same unexpected physical response that had sprung to life aboard the cruise ship. She'd spent the last twenty-one days rationalizing that response, blaming it on the unrealistic romantic atmosphere the ship readily provided. Drunk on fantasy, as her grandmother would say.

Here in Boston, her common sense intact, she should be above such base feelings. That she wasn't now threw her off balance. Ripping open a package of rye crackers, she pointedly changed the subject. "I imagine you'll be glad to fly out of this arctic weather."

"I love snow. Besides, I can't think of a more appropriate place to celebrate the holiday."

"It will be Christmas no matter where you go."

"In Florida?" He shook his head. "Not really. Hang all the decorations you want, but short of a miracle, it's still never going to snow. Hard to find yuletide spirit among palm trees and sand."

She'd thought the same when Shannon had invited her to celebrate Christmas in Nassau. Not that she worried about Christmas, but winter just wasn't winter without snow. Still, where and how Mark spent his holiday wasn't something she should be thinking about now when she needed to remain detached and unemotional.

He settled back in his chair. "I really thought this Christmas would be different, especially when Shannon welcomed me with open arms."

"Shannon has a way of embracing life that will get her into trouble one of these days." Exactly ten days, Celie counted, before Shannon's return. Her roommate meant well, but it seemed best to thwart her enthusiastic matchmaking efforts before they got out of hand.

"She says she listens with her heart, not her ears."

Celie crushed another cracker into a pile of crumbs. "She should have told you I'd changed my mind."

"Stop trying to pass the buck," Mark said. "It was your decision—" He stopped, narrowing his eyes. "It was your decision, wasn't it?"

"Of course. Uneasy as it made her, the edge to his voice certainly was justified. She wondered whether he would feel better knowing she'd cried herself to sleep for a week after she posted the note. What he needed was neither an apology nor a lame explanation, but an assurance he wasn't at fault. "I had our best interests in mind. Nothing personal—"

"Nothing personal?" He leaned forward, resting his elbows on the table. "Three weeks ago we agreed to spend the rest of our lives together, and now you tell me it was nothing personal? Honey, it doesn't get more personal than that."

This was the reaction she'd expected. What she hadn't anticipated was the way her heart twisted at the bitterness in his voice. She bit back an apology, knowing he was too angry to hear it.

His eyes darkened. "Do you know I booked that cruise just to get away from everything? A little R and R, a chance to see life from a new perspective, a time to sit down and plan my future. The morning I met you, you couldn't have taken me down harder if you'd used a cannon."

Celie fiddled with her silverware. Clichéd as it sounded, the earth had rocked for her as well. She could remember every moment, every smell, every sound of that morning. All because she'd found him doing the same thing she liked to do—something Shannon insisted bordered on insanity—standing on deck before dawn to welcome the brilliant Caribbean sunrise.

It seemed inevitable that she would eat breakfast with Mark, natural that things progressed from there until they were inseparable for the remainder of the cruise. The allure of the tropics, she supposed, not to mention the fact she'd wandered a lifetime away from Boston and for a brief time found herself willing to follow her heart.

But one couldn't live life chasing whims. Every day at work she saw firsthand the devastating effects of not considering every angle, not analyzing every potential flaw. While seizing the moment had been a startling yet refreshing change from her ordered life, it certainly wasn't a lifestyle that matched her own.

There wasn't an easy way to explain, and she was grateful when Vera appeared and unknowingly spared her the task of trying.

After unloading her serving tray, Vera hovered near the table to watch Mark stir the stew. He sampled a spoonful, then nodded. "Excellent. Give my compliments to the chef."

Vera beamed. "Don't know what those girls have been feeding you—neither can so much as boil water. Not that they couldn't learn, mind you. I've got cranberry muffins in the oven—call if you need anything." Humming, she ambled back to the kitchen.

"So you can't cook." Mark buttered a thick slice of brown bread. "Any other dark secrets you forgot to mention?"

"Now you know them all," Celie told him, her voice as light and teasing as his. With a little effort, maybe she could keep the remainder of their conversation innocuous.

"I've barely scratched the surface," Mark murmured.

Which was exactly the way she wanted it. Well, maybe not what she wanted, but unquestionably what was best for her—and for him. Best in the way exercise and brussels sprouts were. Painful as she found her decision now, they'd both be better off for it in the long run.

Vera returned to the table bearing a napkin-covered basket of muffins. "Just out of the oven," she warned. Then she once again basked in Mark's smile of approval after he sampled one.

"If you wouldn't mind sharing this recipe," he said, "I'd sure like to send it to my mother."

Vera fluttered her apron. "Not really a recipe—just a little of this, a little of that. I'll jot down what I can."

Celie shook her head as she watched Vera march proudly back to the kitchen. "You've just made a friend for life."

"She's a great judge of character," Mark said, reaching for another muffin. "No wonder she's adopted you."

From his smile, Celie realized he complimented her as well as

Vera. She tried to feel skeptical at flattery rolling so easily from his lips. After all, she'd met her share of sweet talkers who dropped meaningless compliments by the dozen. She just couldn't remember their sounding so sincere or affecting her this way.

Nor could she remember any of the half-dozen harmless topics she'd planned on addressing. For a few moments they ate in silence, just long enough for her to relax, before he spoke. "Why didn't you go to Nassau with Shannon?"

Look what happened the last time I tagged along. Celie shrugged. "I'm on twenty-four-hour call at the center over the holidays. Most of the workers have families, and they appreciate getting a break."

"You have a family," Mark pointed out. "Shannon said she couldn't wait until I meet your grandmother."

Almost choking on a chunk of cucumber, Celie grabbed a glass of ice water and washed it down. Grandmother would eat Mark alive, but since he was leaving Boston in another hour or so, she saw no need to elaborate on Shannon's statement.

It did present a new set of problems. Shannon inevitably waited until the last minute to pack, which shouldn't have given her much time to chat with Mark. However, Celie knew better than to assume. "What else did Shannon say?"

"She wanted to put me in a big box and wrap it for you to open when you arrived home. Said I'd be the best Christmas present she'd ever given you."

Celie smiled wryly. "I'm glad you had enough sense to say no."

"I had to. We couldn't find a big enough box."

She would have tried to chastise him with the same disapproving frown she used whenever Shannon's humor stepped past the bounds of decorum, but his grin made it impossible for her to do anything but laugh.

He and Shannon were two of a kind. Maybe she'd turn the tables on her roommate for once, play matchmaker herself, and raise a glass at their wedding.

The thought made her throat tighten. Dispatching him from her life was one thing; toasting his future with someone else was another thing altogether. Disturbed by the thought, she tackled the salad Vera had laced with ham, turkey, and cheese.

"You know, this is the first real dinner we've eaten together."

He was right. Despite the lavish twenty-four-hour buffet the cruise ship had provided, they'd bribed the steward to pack them picnic baskets of crusty French bread, cheese, fruit, and wine, which they ate in quiet corners of the ship.

That was a lifetime away, Celie reminded herself, a sheer fantasy she'd indulged in for one week. She mustered her resolve to avoid talking about it and, instead, focused the conversation on his career highlights. He answered her questions willingly, and once again she felt herself relax.

Carrying a pot of steaming coffee, Vera appeared at the table. "Fresh-brewed," she assured Mark as she filled his cup. "Ground the beans myself." She set the pot atop a folded napkin and plopped down, uninvited, in an empty chair at the table while she eyed Mark with open curiosity. "So you're sightseeing?"

"Yes, ma'am." Mark looked at Celie.

"A Marine, are you?" Vera asked.

He recoiled at the unintentional insult. "Navy, ma'am."

"A young man like you should be sharing Christmas with his family," Vera chided. "You married?"

He grinned at her blatant interest. "Not yet."

"Not married." Arching her eyebrows, Vera glanced at Celie before asking Mark another question. "Where do you hail from?"

"Arizona, originally, although I'm stationed in Florida. I've always wanted to see a colonial Christmas, and the tour books say Boston is decorated to the hilt this time of year, so I came north."

Vera sniffed. "Best money can buy, I guess." She turned to Celie. "Your family's expectin' you, I imagine. Yesterday's society column had a big to-do about your grandma's upcoming Christmas Ball."

Earlier in the week, Celie'd been interviewed by phone but hadn't yet found time to read the subsequent article. The newspapers always managed to make the ball sound like some glitzy affair, playing down the fact it netted thousands of dollars for local charities. Squirming under Mark's inquisitive gaze, she changed the subject. "What are you doing for Christmas, Vera?"

"Helpin' the gals cook turkeys down at the homeless shelter." Vera stood and piled the emptied dishes. "Guess you're ready for dessert."

She rarely turned down Vera's desserts, but tonight Celie was more interested in escaping the cross-examination she knew lay ahead. Sometimes Vera's matchmaking attempts could put Shannon's to shame, and judging from the way she eyed Mark, she intended to move things along best she could.

No doubt about it, it was time to leave. Celie folded her napkin and checked her watch. "Vera, dinner was great, but we really have to go."

Her protest fell on deaf ears. A minute later Vera produced two generous slices of pie topped with melted cheddar cheese.

"Don't bother arguin'," Vera said, placing one plate before Celie, the other before Mark. "Apples are what's good for you. This is my secret recipe, and there's plenty more. So, Commander, how long have you known Celie—"

Interrupted by a customer pushing through the door, Vera sighed. "Be right back," she said, leaving to seat the newcomer.

Thanking fate for small favors, Celie finished her pie in record time, and when Vera returned, she requested the check.

Vera shook her head. "No check, don't bother fussin' about it, either. This is the only Christmas present you'll get from me this year." Wiping her hands on a clean corner of her apron, she smiled at Mark. "Nice meetin' you, Commander. How long you stayin' in Boston?"

"We're on our way to the airport now." Celie answered for him.

"Not tonight you ain't. Runways closed 'cause of the storm, the radio said. You two take care out there."

Radio announcers were sometimes wrong, Celie assured herself as she pulled on her coat. Even if the airport did close, once the runway crews plowed, salted, sanded, or ashed, the planes would be running again.

Outside, she felt as if she'd stepped onto another planet. The wind had gentled, teasing the snow into gauzy clouds that shrouded the light from the overhead lamps and lent an eerie, milky glow to the street.

"Reminds me of my days at Annapolis." Gathering a handful of snow, Mark packed it into a ball, then pitched it against a street sign. He turned, surveying the line of trees along the street, their bare branches silhouetted against the inky sky. "Looks like one of those glass globes you shake to make snow fall inside. I grew up wishing for real winters."

And when he came north, his Academy classmates envied him for growing up on a ranch, as if horses and cacti could hold a candle to the untamed energy of a snowstorm.

Mindless of his spit-polished shoes, he waded through a foot-high drift blocking the sidewalk, making a path for Celie.

So far, she'd been polite to a fault. Still, unless he handled things with infinite care, he knew he'd spend the night dozing on one of the vinyl airport chairs.

On his incoming flight, the attendant had warned that the impending blizzard might make flying out of Boston difficult for a few days. While passengers around him grumbled, he'd accepted it as a sign that fate stood by his side. So far, so good.

Too bad the right moment to tackle the lettergram hadn't arisen during dinner. Judging from the once-over Vera had given him before she decided he might be suitable company for Celie, he felt it would have been safer to tangle with a mother bear defending her cub than incur Celie's wrath in front of Vera.

Besides, this was a personal matter, one that didn't require the interference of a third party, no matter how loving or well-intentioned she was.

He could blurt out a confession now and pray Celie would pity him and allow him to stay the night, if not outright change her mind. A self-defeating idea if he ever had one; he could imagine her shoving him face-first into the nearest snowbank and marching home without a second look his way. And he knew it would be no less than he deserved.

Prudence demanded he adopt a more cautious approach. Prod a little, defuse her arguments one by one, until she came to know what he'd realized from the start: They were destined to meet, to fall in love, to marry.

She walked with a purpose, he realized, and he tried to distract her, to delay the evening's end. "Where are all those things they show on greeting cards? The holly trees, the cardinals, the carolers?"

"This is a conservative neighborhood. We make do with electric candles in the window, red bows on the lampposts."

She was right, he saw. Every window up and down the street boasted a single lit candle. Every house except hers. Maybe he'd go out later and buy a few Christmas things to scatter around her house, if the malls hadn't closed because of the storm. He studied the snowdrifts sweeping across the street. "How high will those get?"

She stopped and considered. "A few feet, maybe. Doesn't matter; the plows should go through before long. Even if they don't, my car has four-wheel drive."

Under the shadowy streetlamp, her eyes resembled warm jade. Whoever taught her how to hide her feelings behind them hadn't quite succeeded, he thought. Since he'd arrived he'd glimpsed emotions he knew she didn't want him to see. Confusion. Desire. And maybe, just maybe, a yearning to see whether her impulsive behavior aboard ship had been based on something other than sheer boredom.

He wondered how she could look more desirable now bundled in a quilted ski jacket than she had in a bathing suit aboard the ship. *Look, don't touch.* He remembered his vow even as he reached for her.

He picked up another handful of snow instead, knowing without a doubt the next few days were going to be the longest ones in his life.

Celie watched him sift snow through his fingers. That a man who'd sailed around the world countless times would be fascinated by a mere snowfall amazed her. She'd always liked winter but hadn't really stopped to admire its raw beauty since she'd been a child and too young to know there were more important matters to consider. Now she took a moment and tried to view the street through his eyes.

Snow covered everything in sight, softening the no-nonsense lines of the homes lining the street, lending a surreal quality to the night. Around her the world looked new, a winter paradise touched only by the footsteps they'd just made.

She shook away the foolishly romantic thought. What she saw was a section of a city grinding to a sudden halt because an arctic snowstorm swooped down from the north. As beautiful as the snow might seem, it most likely had closed Logan Airport. She found nothing peaceful about that.

Too soon, it seemed, they'd reached her house. She stopped at the Subaru to retrieve the can of de-icer. Instead of experiencing relief because the evening was drawing to a close, she felt herself droop with disappointment. Lack of sleep combined with anxiety about the upcoming holiday had nudged her emotions out of sync. Tonight, she didn't crave quiet, she welcomed company. And not just any company would do, she thought, glancing sidelong at Mark.

Inside her foyer she shrugged off her coat and draped it on the antique brass hall tree, then found an empty hook for Mark. When he ducked his head to shake away the snow caked to the hem of his pants, she saw flakes of snow melting into droplets in his black hair.

"You should have worn a hat," she scolded, brushing them away. "Your hair is wet."

He trapped her hand with his, holding it against his cheek as he straightened. She stood too close, she realized when his thighs brushed hers. Instead of moving away, she held her breath while he lifted his other hand and traced her mouth with his thumb.

"Your lips are blue," he whispered, giving her ample time to pull away, to protest.

She did neither, her gaze held captive to his as he drew her closer. Anticipation made her heady, tightened her muscles even as it weakened her knees. One kiss, she promised herself. Just one, to make the parting sweet.

His hands, cool against her skin, cradled her face before their lips met. His mouth brushed hers, tantalizing, promising as much or as little as she wanted. Without considering what she wanted, she rose on her tiptoes to bring her mouth to his.

She forgot the world around her, aware only of herself and Mark. Instinctively knowing he was everything she'd ever wanted, ever needed, she lost herself in the headiness of the kiss, in his mouth, which teased and tantalized and, without words, urged her closer.

An addicting sensation, as dangerous as the illicit drugs used by some of the women who sought help at the center where she worked. Temporarily satisfying and exhilarating but, in the long run, devastating to body and soul. It took every ounce of her dwindling self-control to step away, to lift a hand to smooth her hair while she searched for some excuse for her inexcusable behavior. She found none.

After quickly tugging off her boots, she walked past Mark into the living room and switched on the overhead light she seldom used. Much as she hated its garish glow, it banished any trace of warmth from the room. Since she couldn't count on common sense to keep her out of trouble, she had no choice but to rely on external measures. She reminded herself once again that she was doing what would be best for them both.

He stood at the doorway watching her as she batted away a strand of hair clinging to her cheek. "You shouldn't have done that." Her voice trembled, effectively negating the accusation.

"No, I shouldn't have."

His agreement flustered her. By right he could assert she'd been as willing as he, that she'd made the overture by touching him, by staying a moment too long in the cozy foyer.

The fact that he didn't made her even more aware of her indiscretion. She'd known there'd be trouble the moment he'd walked down her stairway. She should have called a cab then and there. Better late than never, she thought as she walked across the room and pulled the phone book from a desk drawer. "I'll see if you can catch a flight out tonight."

"Vera said the airport's closed," he reminded her.

"Maybe Vera's wrong." She looked up the number, then dialed. Yes, the airport was closed, an obscenely cheerful receptionist told her. Runways were iced over, all flights delayed until further notice, call again in the morning.

Three

Celie slowly replaced the receiver as she toyed with options. There had been a certain security in knowing he would be gone when morning came, even though she knew she'd regret waking to find herself alone. Still, he'd be back where he belonged and her life could proceed on its normal course.

She didn't have to repeat the airport receptionist's conversation for Mark. She could tell by his grin that he'd clearly read the expression on her face.

"No problem," he said, taking the phone book from her. Flipping through the pages, he found the hotel listings, then made several calls. After the eighth, he looked at her and shrugged. "No vacancies. Apparently I'm not the only one stranded in Boston tonight. Sorry to inconvenience you further, but would you mind putting me up for the night?"

He didn't sound sorry at all, and his cocky smile sent her heart into a somersault. Trying to tamp down an absurd suspicion that he'd somehow manipulated the weather, she considered his request. She could send him to the Ritz-Carlton to one of the suites her family reserved for business guests.

Not a good idea, she immediately decided. Inevitably her family would find out, and Mark's appearance was one she'd find difficult to explain, especially since she hadn't revealed her betrothal and subsequent change of mind to anyone but Shannon. "I don't have a guest bedroom," she told him, "but you're welcome to use the sofa."

Even as she spoke, she realized the sofa was easily half a foot too short for him to sleep comfortably there. "On second thought, since Shannon invited you in, I'm sure she wouldn't mind your using her room while she's gone."

"Look, I don't want to put anyone out," Mark said graciously. "I figured a place this big would have a guest room or two."

"It would, except Shannon keeps her model train collection upstairs in one room, and we share the other for office space."

He still seemed hesitant to accept her invitation, and she wondered whether he'd been counting on the evening to draw to an end, too. "If that's not accommodating enough, I could make a few more phone calls," she offered. "There must be a vacancy somewhere; Boston has plenty of hotels."

"Society columns, too."

She blinked, trying to follow his train of thought. "What does that mean?"

"Shannon said you hadn't announced our engagement. Certainly the gossipmongers of Boston would be interested in meeting the man Cecilia Hargrave Mason agreed to marry. Or refused to marry."

Celie could feel the faint push of her pulse behind her eyes, a warning of an impending tension headache. "The papers don't publish broken engagements."

Except the tabloids, which would have a field day. HEIRESS BREAKS SAILOR'S HEART. Cringing at the imaginary headline, she wondered what other trivia her roommate had felt obliged to reveal. "While we're on the subject, what else did Shannon tell you about me?"

"Let's see." Mark sorted through magazines stacked on the coffee table until he found the one he wanted. "You were featured in a 'Boston's most eligible bachelorette' article a few months ago."

Rushed as Shannon must have been packing for her vacation, she'd apparently found sufficient time to chat. "In case she forgot to mention it," Celie pointed out, "she engineered that article to drum up publicity for the Resource Center's bachelorette auction."

Mark watched her wriggle her stockinged toes against the plush carpet as she leafed through the magazine pages. He stopped to study a photograph of her receiving her law degree in a hall named after her grandfather. "She also told me your ancestors came over on the Mayflower."

During the cruise she'd refused to mention her wealth or her social ties. Apparently Shannon had seen fit this morning to dangle both in front of him. "Everyone's ancestors immigrated from somewhere."

"But everyone's descendants don't own three-fourths of Boston."

"It's hardly three-fourths."

He tossed the magazine back on the coffee table before he settled onto the sofa. "You don't have to apologize for being rich."

"Of course I don't. I never have. The reason I didn't mention it . . ." She stopped, trying to think of a way to explain it. "For once, I just wanted to blend in with the crowd."

"It didn't work. You stood out like a sore thumb, and your money had nothing to do with it."

How could he make such a mundane comment sound like sheer adulation? She gave a little laugh, trying to sound bored. "My aura, I suppose."

"You could call it that," he said amiably. He watched her tuck her legs underneath her as she sat on the opposite end of the leather sofa. "You could also move a little closer."

At his soft words her breath hitched. *Watch it,* she told herself, realizing he'd switched on the magnetic charm that had captivated her aboard ship—charm that she could and should well resist here on her home ground. Tempting as his invitation sounded, the encounter in the foyer had taught her to keep her distance. "I'm comfortable right here."

"Warm enough?"

She hated the way the laughter threading his voice softened her resistance. Before another minute passed, she needed to establish boundaries for them both. "I hope you didn't misunderstand my invitation to stay overnight. It's for room and board only."

"Of course."

"And that kiss in the foyer—it didn't mean . . ." She heard him chuckle while she struggled to finish the sentence. "You know what I mean," she said, glaring because he could have said he knew what she meant and saved her the awkward moment.

"You mean kissing me a few minutes ago didn't mean anything."

"Exactly."

"Just like the week aboard the ship didn't mean anything."

He'd caught her off guard again. Foolish of her to assume the issue had been settled. She lifted her chin defensively but fought to keep her voice calm, averse to having him know she'd relived those days over and over, more times than necessary. "I wouldn't trade that week for anything in the world, but it wasn't real. I—we both just needed something different—"

"An interlude?"

She winced at the impersonal word. "Let's say I was swept away by the atmosphere. It wasn't something I'd ever done before, and I'm certain it's something I'll never do again."

He sat still, analyzing her with a look she couldn't begin to read. When the silence pricked at her conscience, she spoke again. "I know how these things go. In a few months, we'd be bored with each other and both searching for a way out. It would be better for us both to call it quits now, while we're still friends."

"How could you know what's better for me?"

The anger she'd expected earlier surfaced now. She'd been naive to think he wouldn't harbor bad feelings, and she'd be a fool not to understand why he would. "I'm sorry—"

"Stop saying that," he snapped.

After the week they'd shared, obviously there was no way he could divorce himself from memories and establish a platonic relationship. Part of her wanted to say it was time for him to go, that he could spend the night at the airport until he caught the first available flight south.

But it was a holiday season, Logan's busiest. No doubt all flights to anywhere would be booked solid, and he might end up celebrating Christmas with a group of stranded strangers. Against her better judgment she heard herself saying, "If you're really intent on seeing Boston, you're welcome to stay here for a few days."

He leaned against the sofa back and considered her offer. "I don't want to intrude," he finally told her in a voice that said he was sorely tempted.

"You won't." She'd make sure of it. "I'll be at work most of the time anyhow. I'll lend you Shannon's house key so you can come and go as you wish. There's just one thing I ask in return—you don't breathe a word to anyone that we were engaged."

"When's the big ball?"

She frowned at the unrelated question. "Did you hear what I said? I want a promise."

"Scout's honor," he murmured, flashing the smile she found herself liking more and more. "The ball Vera mentioned—when is it, Christmas Eve?"

"Tomorrow night. Why?"

"This is the only set of dress blues I packed. Is there a dry cleaner nearby?"

"The ball is by invitation *only.*" She stressed the last word.

"You already have an escort?"

Admitting she didn't might prove unwise; saying she did would be an outright lie. She tried to brush off his question. "I don't think that has anything to do with—"

"No, it doesn't. I'm just curious about the chap who replaced me."

"Chap?" Hating the way her voice rose, she swallowed and drew a deep breath. She wasn't fickle, and she needed him to see that. "No one has replaced you. You're not going because you weren't invited."

"Couldn't you invite me?"

He couldn't possibly know what he was asking. Exposing him to her grandmother would only court trouble; telling him so would probably court more. "I serve as hostess. It would be grossly unfair to invite you along and then ignore you the rest of the evening while I tend to my duties."

He seemed to be listening to her one-sided reasoning with growing interest. Searching for a stronger argument to dissuade him, she added, "Besides, my grandmother drafts the guest list."

"The grandmother Shannon can't wait for me to meet?"

She considered explaining that her roommate's remark had been a veiled warning, but that would involve an extensive description of her grandmother's character and inevitably lead to more questions.

It would be best, Celie finally decided as she stood, to simply abandon the subject. "I need to finish some work I brought home. You're welcome to watch television, if you want."

He watched her instead. As usual, she sat on the living room floor and spread her files around her on the rug, since it served as a more comfortable space than her antique roll-top desk upstairs. She could feel his gaze on the back of her neck when she bent over the first file and began penciling in the margins.

Years ago she'd learned to concentrate in the noisiest atmosphere, a tactic that allowed her to accomplish considerable work by utilizing a few minutes here and there. Tonight, though, she found herself reading the same paragraph again and again, concentrating not on the facts and documented evidence before her, but on the man sitting in her living room.

An hour later, she gathered the files together and returned them to her briefcase. In the time she'd normally handle a half-dozen files, she hadn't managed to peruse one. She couldn't blame Mark; he hadn't said a word. The fault rested solely with her overactive imagination. Despite her best intentions, her mind seemed determined to replay the week they'd shared, one precious moment at a time.

And though it didn't matter in the least, she wondered whether he was recalling the same. Snapping shut her briefcase, she glanced at him. Whatever he was thinking, she couldn't tell from his shuttered expression or his half smile; for all she knew, he could be reviewing military maneuvers.

Too tense to be tired, she still checked her watch when she stood. If she pretended to be exhausted, she could call it a night and slip upstairs. There, alone, she'd have a fighting chance to gather her wits and whatever else she needed to get back on track. "I'll put fresh sheets on Shannon's bed."

"I can make my own bed." Mark switched off the living room light before he followed her up the stairs. After retrieving his duffel bag from the bathroom, he took the flannel sheets Celie'd pulled from the hall closet.

She should touch him just to prove mere physical contact didn't send her senses spinning. "There's cold cereal in the cupboard above the stove," she said, lacing her fingers behind her back.

He nodded but stayed where he was, blocking the hallway. She waited a moment for him to move, and when he didn't, dropped a subtle hint. "Is there anything else you need?"

"How 'bout a good-night kiss?"

In a house with nine rooms, she certainly could manage to be somewhere he wasn't. She had to remember to keep her distance; this close to him, her mind started reeling as if she'd downed several shots of bourbon. "Thanks, but I'll have to pass this time."

He leaned closer. "It's mighty cold outside."

Flirting again, she told herself, but his whisper seemed to curl around her, its combination of amusement and desire making her heart race. "I have an electric blanket and a quilt."

"Suppose the storm knocks out the power?"

"There's a working fireplace in my bedroom." She wanted to prove she was practical, but the erotic possibilities of sharing an evening lit only by a flickering fire whetted her senses until she could barely breathe.

"Sounds better than Caribbean moonlight," he murmured, and she had to silently agree. Memories that had kept her awake night after night once again crowded into her mind.

He knew; she could tell by the way his eyes mirrored her own desire. She also knew the advantage was his; if he reached for her, she'd be lost. But he kept hold of the bed linens in one hand, the duffel in the other, and stayed where he was. "Which room is Shannon's?"

He had to repeat the question before she found the presence of mind to nod toward the doorway next to hers.

"Good night, Celie." He brushed a kiss on her forehead before he walked past her.

Once he heard Celie's bedroom door click shut, Mark sat on the mattress and dug a sheet of paper from his pocket. So much for his good intentions to mention the lettergram this evening. The right moment had never arrived. She'd been so intent on finishing her work he didn't dare bother her, just sat there watching her while he silently rehearsed several opening lines. When he'd finally settled on the best one, she'd rushed up the stairs.

He fingered the creased paper and listened to the sounds in the bedroom next door. Tomorrow at breakfast, he promised his nagging conscience. He'd rise early, maybe make one of his mother's special omelettes stuffed with onions and chili peppers. Then he'd offer his confession, establish a bond of trust by telling the truth, and let fate take charge.

Then again, he couldn't help but wonder whether telling the truth might be partly to blame for the circumstances he found himself in now. Aboard ship he'd felt compelled to tell her everything about himself, and that included a string of broken engagements. Five, to be exact, over the last twenty years, from women who were terminally nice, extremely compatible, everything a man could wish for in a wife.

Long naval tours, constant base reassignments—he'd seen both work together to ruin relationships, yet deep down he knew neither really precluded marriage, although they were the reasons he extended to each woman when he realized he couldn't go through with marriage. Amicable partings, each and every one, with only a twinge of regret that he hadn't yet found the right woman.

Only one in the world was meant for him, his grandmother always said, and it was up to him to find her. The moment he'd met Celie, he realized his grandmother spoke the truth.

Maybe Celie, in an attempt to cushion herself in case he changed his mind down the road, found it easier to pull away now—if that's what she thought she was doing. He had no doubt that had he dropped the flowered sheets and reached for her, she'd be sharing his bed right now.

Much as his body insisted otherwise, it had been wise to resist that impulse. More than passion, he wanted to see trust light her eyes. She'd been willing aboard ship to go where fate led her, and that had been right into his arms. Now he needed to convince her she was predestined to remain there a lifetime, not just one week.

Next door a floorboard creaked. A drawer slid open, slid shut.

He was on her territory now, and he needed to proceed with caution. If things didn't work out, he had the feeling he'd be hit with far worse than a Dear John letter.

He stripped the sheets from the canopied bed and remade it. Definitely Shannon's room, he thought, eyeing the overabundance of eyelet and lace, the clutter of childhood mementoes. Nets suspended from each corner housed a menagerie of stuffed animals, and paperbacks crowded on a bookshelf against the far wall shared space with a collection of dolls.

He'd glanced into the other bedroom when he came upstairs earlier and had found it decorator designed in pastels. Military neat, a place for everything, everything in its place. It wouldn't hurt to splash a little red paint on those cream-colored walls, he decided, tucking the lettergram back in his duffel.

It was now silent next door. She was probably asleep, but he couldn't resist rapping on the wall. "Sweet dreams."

She didn't dare answer. Since she'd returned home from the cruise, her dreams had been anything but sweet. Some left her miserably aroused; others portrayed a life she'd never live, content at Mark's side, rearing dark-haired, blue-eyed children.

The dreams weren't her fault. Entertaining thoughts of what might have been led her unconscious mind to create fantasies into larger-than-life proportions. She had no excuse for the thoughts she entertained during the days, when she was wide-awake sober, and wise enough to know better.

She didn't want to hurt his feelings, but knew she needed to tend to her own. Tomorrow she'd tell him flat out, plain and simple: It wasn't love that brought them together, but the lethal combination of moonlight and wine and visions of happily ever after.

He'd just been in the right place at the wrong time.

She'd start by explaining how she'd only half-heartedly toyed with the idea of the singles' cruise when Shannon first proposed it. How Grandmother Grace's horrified protest—"It's just not something *we* do"—spurred her into purchasing a ticket.

How aboard ship she found herself doing the improbable. Stargazing while snuggled against Mark's chest. Sipping chilled chardonnay straight from the bottle. Considering possibilities and promises for a future that would never be—could never be.

Fairy-tale-cruise mentality. She realized that now, although at the time what she did seemed as natural as her spontaneous agreement to marry Mark after he'd completed his final Navy tour. She'd whispered yes without stopping to consider every angle, without weighing both sides of the issue.

Without acting like a Hargrave.

That single, reckless moment in her life had now returned to haunt her—in person.

She buried her face in the pillow and tried to look at the bright side. Suppose she'd married him on the spur of the moment and ended up as one of those clinging, tear-stained wives crowded at the base when the sub loaded. She'd need more now than a letter-gram to dissolve the relationship. She'd be up to her neck in legal fees and lawyers, not to mention the publicity and the well-meaning counsel from her family.

Tugging her blanket higher, she tucked it under her chin. Despite her unwavering resolution to take matters in hand in the morning, sleep was a long time coming.

Celie heard the phone ring when she stepped out of the shower. Her instinctive reaction to grab a towel and dash to answer it was fast aborted by Mark's deep and disgustingly wide-awake voice drifting up the stairs.

After pulling her robe from the porcelain wall hook, she slipped it on and belted it around her waist, then wrapped her wet hair turban-style in a towel as she hurried down the stairs.

"Here she is now." Mark flashed an engaging smile when she snatched the receiver away.

"Hello?" She tried to dodge his fingers as they pushed an errant strand of wet hair beneath the towel, then absentmindedly batted away his hand when it lingered to trace a path over her jaw.

"Cecilia? Are you all right?" Grandmother Grace's elegant voice rang with suspicion.

"Of course." Celie glared at Mark, who lounged nearby, shamelessly eavesdropping, then turned away.

"When that man answered the phone, I thought . . ." Her grandmother's voice trailed away, for the moment unwilling to elaborate on the horrible possibilities.

Celie rushed a reassurance before the inevitable questions began. "I'm fine, Grandmother. How are you?"

"Busy. Tonight's seating arrangements must be changed since Congressman Coffey called to say he'll be attending without an escort. I've instructed the caterer to fit an extra setting at the head table, unless you have an objection."

Even if she did, Celie knew it wouldn't matter. The call was merely a formality to announce a decision her grandmother had already made. "That's fine. I'll see you tonight, Grandmother."

Without giving the woman an opportunity to cross-examine her about Mark, Celie replaced the receiver. She turned around, intending to tell him her recorder would answer the phone if she couldn't, then stopped in mid-thought.

Leaning against the wall, he watched her, his arms crossed over his chest. His western-cut jeans clung to sinewy thighs. Casually dressed, he looked just as devastatingly handsome as he had last night in his dress blues.

"Something wrong?" he asked.

Suddenly aware of how little she wore, she drew the collar of her robe shut. "Just a last-minute change in tonight's plans."

"Ah, yes, the big ball." He moved so casually it took her a few seconds to realize he was closing the distance between them. "If it's been canceled, maybe you could give me a nighttime tour of the city."

"It's not canceled." He stood a foot taller, and her initial instinct was to take a step back. But she refused to be intimidated. "Grandmother called to say she's seating Charlie Coffey by my side for dinner.

"The congressman?" Mark whistled. "What is your political preference, by the way?"

The buttons at the neckline of his chambray shirt were unfastened, and the open collar revealed some of the dark hair sprinkled over his chest. She remembered how it had tickled her cheek when she'd rested her head . . .

She whipped her gaze back to his face when his question finally seeped into her brain. "What difference does that make?"

"I'd peg you to be a Democrat, and unless memory serves me wrong, Coffey's Republican. That could make for some interesting media coverage should you someday become the First Lady."

Her blood sugar must be sinking to an all-time low. It certainly wasn't his smile that sent her heart racing as if she'd just finished the marathon. She headed toward the kitchen to find something to calm her jittery pulse. "When I make it to the White House, it will be as President," she said over her shoulder. "My grandmother would stand for nothing less."

"I didn't get a chance to talk much with her, but I take it she isn't the typical gray-haired darling rocking away in her porch swing?"

"Before she turned twenty she marched for women's right to vote. She hasn't sat down since." Celie frowned at the table set for two, then at Mark, who moved around her kitchen with a too-familiar ease. "You aren't going to eat Cheerios with a fork?"

"We aren't going to eat Cheerios, period. It's time you tasted the famous Edwards's omelette."

Celie checked the clock over the sink. "It's time I dressed for work. If you're searching for eggs, I don't have any."

Looking disappointed, Mark closed the refrigerator door. "This is Saturday," he reminded her. "Can't you take a few hours off and show me around your fair city?"

Despite her intentions to put her cards on the table this morning, she needed more time to fine-tune her admission of guilt. Before she told him anything, she needed to make sure there were no loose ends he could unravel.

Besides, she'd find it impossible to deliver a solemn, serious speech while munching cereal. "Problems don't just disappear on weekends. The center is open three hundred sixty-five days a year, twenty-four hours a day, and today I'm on call. If you want to sightsee, take my car. I'm walking to work."

He frowned. "It must be zero degrees outside. I'll drop you off."

It was two below; the radio weatherman had announced the temperature just after her alarm went off. To someone used to sun and surf, she supposed that sounded intolerable, but she enjoyed the cold. "I always walk. Most days it's the only chance I have to exercise. There's a map of Boston in the top desk drawer, if you want it."

He pocketed the spare car and house keys she handed him. "You'll need your car for the dance tonight, won't you? What time should I be back?"

"Don't worry. Grandmother's sending her chauffeur. She can't stand the thought of my Subaru parked next to her Bentley."

He laughed as if he thought she was joking. "What time should I expect you home?"

"After midnight. I'll try not to wake you when I come in." She glanced at the clock again. Ten minutes late already; no time to grab a bowl of cereal. Just as well, she decided as she left the kitchen. The last thing she needed to do was sit and chat with someone who'd soon be flying out of her life.

While scanning the menu, Mark looked up when someone tapped him on the shoulder.

"These listings are for ordinary folk," Vera told him, plucking the menu from his hands. "Tell me what you want, and I'll make it for you."

Mark sniffed. "What's that I smell?"

"Cinnamon rolls. Just pulled them from the oven."

He drew in another deep breath. "Bet they're as good as the ones my mom makes."

"I'll dab some extra icing on a few for you. Where's Celie?"

"Working."

Vera clucked like a worried mother hen. "Leavin' you all to yourself?"

"I'm a big boy," Mark assured her. "She lent me her car so I can look around the city."

"Plenty of sites, if that's what you like. You and Celie been friends long?"

"We met a few weeks ago during a Thanksgiving cruise."

Vera pursed her lips. "Figure the airport's open now. You flyin' out today?'."

Sensing a purpose behind her cross-examination, he prayed he'd come out on the winning side. "I've decided to stay awhile."

"Good." She hesitated a moment, twisting the corner of her apron around her fingers. "Things will work out," she finally said. "I just feel it in my bones."

He arched his eyebrows. "What things?"

"I've watched that girl mope around for the last three weeks. Only one thing makes a grown woman act that way."

He prayed Vera's two-bit psychology was accurate. Although he had the feeling he could enlist her help, he'd promised Celie his silence. "Do you have fresh coffee to go with those rolls?"

In her old bedroom in the Hargrave mansion, Celie stepped into her emerald-green ball gown. Sweeping her hair from her face with a jeweled comb, she let her curls cascade over her bared shoulders. Heirloom earrings, webs of gold studded with emeralds and diamonds, matched her locket and the band she fastened around her wrist. After a final glance in the mirror, she pulled on her sandals, then swept down the front staircase and into the ballroom.

The ceiling-length windows lining the far wall were strung with miniature blinking white lights and draped with red velvet bunting. A cedar tree laden with six generations of family ornaments towered in the center of the room beneath a crystal chandelier sporting sprigs of holly and mistletoe.

She watched her family gather around a cascading fountain of punch centered on the refreshment table. Nothing's changed, she thought. Every year they argued about the carved-ice swan, whether it should go in the center of the table or next to—

"The punch." Being the eldest had its advantages. Grandmother Grace's decision was immediately enacted by the uniformed staff. She watched Celie cross the room and offered a powdered cheek for her to kiss. "You look very pretty, dear. Katherine's been waiting for you."

"Hello, Mother. Merry Christmas." Smiling, Celie brushed a kiss on her mother's cheek.

Katherine returned her smile and checked her watch. "We were about to form the reception line without you, Celie."

Forty minutes later, Celie's hands and feet ached. She'd learned long ago to avoid wearing rings, since every handshake became a prelude to agony, driving precious stones into tender skin. But she had enough blue blood coursing in her veins to keep from pairing walking shoes with her ball gown.

Would she still be standing here when she was eighty-four, Celie wondered, like her grandmother? Ramrod straight, displaying family jewelry hidden in a lard bucket during the Revolutionary War, her grandmother refused the aid of her cane while she welcomed guests.

More likely, Celie thought, she'd follow in Louise's footsteps. Her great-aunt drooped from the strain of preparation, but perched on a Duncan-Phyfe chair, she chatted with guests, blatantly ignoring her sister's looks of withering disapproval.

One hundred and six, Celie counted as she greeted another couple and urged them toward her grandmother. Since Grandmother limited the guest list to 125 coveted invitations, the line had to be nearing an end.

Flexing her fingers, Celie readied her smile to greet the next guest her mother presented.

"You know the congressman, of course," her mother said.

"Celie, you look positively radiant!" Charlie gripped her hands, then leaned forward and kissed her.

"Thank you, Charlie." Trying not to flinch at his hearty voice, Celie lowered hers in subtle suggestion. "You're looking well yourself." Pulling her hands free she tried to steer him toward her grandmother, but he didn't budge.

"Meet a good friend of mine," he insisted.

Celie blinked and fingered her locket. Whether from lack of sound sleep the night before or from her own imagination working overtime, some absurd illusion caused his guest to resemble . . .

"Commander Mark Edwards." Mark introduced himself while reaching for Celie's hand.

Four

"The commander worried about attending without an invitation, but I assured him you wouldn't mind. This is his first trip to Boston; show him a good time, Celie." Charlie didn't wait for her response before he continued down the reception line.

Aware that her grandmother's glare held even more disapproval than her own, Celie disengaged her fingers from Mark's. "A friend of Charlie's is always welcome here," she said, praying she sounded sincere. "I hope you enjoy the ball, Commander."

"I certainly will," Mark assured her.

Attempting what she hoped passed as a polite smile instead of a panicked grimace, she turned. "Grandmother, Aunt Louise, may I present—"

"Commander Edwards." Mark's southwestern drawl thickened as he spoke. "Charmin' place you've got here, ladies."

"Thank you," Grandmother said stiffly, ignoring his outstretched hand.

When Louise offered a smile, Mark leaned to murmur something too low for Celie to hear. Her great-aunt laughed and patted his hand. Knowing it would be inexcusable to desert the reception line, Celie tried to summon enthusiasm over the remaining couples her mother introduced and dutifully exchanged small talk while she tracked Mark's progress around the ballroom.

Time seemed to trickle past before she greeted the last guest in line. Concealing her impatience, she retrieved Grandmother's cane from behind the French door and admired the decorating efforts her mother had earlier supervised. All the while, the fact that Mark stood just a few feet away gnawed at her mind.

Tapping her cane against the floor, Grandmother surveyed the room. "It appears the congressman found an escort after all."

Celie nodded, her gaze trained on Mark. She found little comfort in the fact that the crowd would permit her to keep her distance, although she reminded herself he'd promised to keep their broken engagement a secret. Certainly she could trust him.

What choice did she have?

"You shouldn't have permitted a stranger into the ball, Katherine." Grandmother's voice became more brittle with every word as she chastised her daughter. "We don't know anything about him. He could be after the Revere candlesticks the reporter insisted on describing for that article in the Sunday paper."

"Good heavens, Grace, he's a career officer in the Navy." Louise rose and straightened her shoulders. "Besides, he's a friend of Charlie's."

Grandmother sniffed. "Anyone with a vote is a friend of the congressman's."

The sisters locked gazes. Grandmother surrendered first, fluttering her hand to signal an end to the confrontation, but Celie caught the suspicious glare she shot across the room. No mistaking its target—in the sea of dinner jackets and tuxedos, Mark stood a head taller than most men around him.

"I never forget a voice," Grandmother muttered to no one in particular. "I've spoken to that man before." The lines on her forehead deepened as she struggled to remember.

Forestalling trouble, Celie rushed to thwart her grandmother's concentration. "You look hot. Let me get you a glass of sherry," she offered.

"First, I'm going to warn Leon to keep a close eye on the guests." Grandmother marched toward a security guard posted inconspicuously behind a swath of holiday bunting.

"Silly old woman." Speaking loudly enough for her retreating sister to hear, Louise then smiled at Celie. "I think the commander is delightful. He said I remind him of his own grandma."

Celie swallowed a groan. Grandmother excelled in snobbery; she'd have nothing to do with Mark because his name didn't appear in the city's elite social register. Aunt Louise, on the other hand, relished taking a stand opposite her sister's, regardless of the subject involved. If Grandmother fussed enough, Louise might become Mark's staunchest ally.

Realizing one could be as bad as the other, Celie abandoned her initial plan to sidestep Mark the remainder of the evening. If nothing else, she needed to keep him off her grandmother's suspicious mind. How could she explain Mark's early-morning presence in her apartment? How would he explain it?

Drifting across the room, Celie paused to trade pleasantries with guests while she tailed Mark. She stayed far enough behind to avoid being obvious, yet close enough to catch snatches of his conversation.

Yes, the weather was definitely a change from Florida sunshine. Yes, he'd graduated from Annapolis. No, he hadn't yet seen much of Boston, but he certainly looked forward to the opportunity.

She relaxed as she heard not a word about the cruise, not a hint regarding the reason he'd shown up at her doorstep.

He hadn't even glanced her way.

Charlie, on the other hand, dogged her. She avoided him as long as she could, already knowing what he planned to say. He'd used the same line for the past ten years.

"How about a dance for old times' sake?" When he finally caught her by the arm, she had little choice but to acquiesce and follow him to the parquet dance floor. There, ignoring the orchestra's underlying beat, he set his own rhythm so he could chat with the constituents around him.

To protect her toes, Celie tried to match his pace. She only needed a few minutes on the dance floor with him to realize she'd never be a politician's wife, at least not Charlie Coffey's wife. A man who couldn't spare a few moments' interest during a dance would be a miserable excuse for a husband.

Don't call the kettle black, she scolded herself, realizing as they circled the floor that her thoughts kept returning to Mark. Only, she rationalized stubbornly, because her grandmother stalked him, waiting for him to make some move to justify her distrust.

A photographer brandishing a camera materialized at the edge of the dance floor. A scheduled photo opportunity, Celie realized with dismay, when Charlie looked down at her and smiled as if they were engaged in intimate conversation. "Hope you don't mind," he murmured.

No doubt the picture would appear in tomorrow's paper with a nonsensical paragraph about her once again being the congressman's romantic interest. Anyone who chose to remember that Charlie and she had battled head-to-head earlier in the year regarding funding cuts for the shelter would know better.

When the photographer disappeared, Charlie promptly ignored her and resumed his public relations campaign. With the upcoming election year, he had his House of Representatives seat to maintain.

She'd lost sight of Mark. Although she smiled and traded social patter with people around her, her gaze continued to comb the crowd. Maybe he'd left, she told herself, wondering why she felt regret instead of relief at the idea.

When the song ended, she thanked Charlie and headed off the floor before he could insist on another dance. Someone caught her by the arm before she'd gotten far. "May I?"

As much as his touch, Mark's voice caused her skin to tingle. Alone in the dark one night aboard ship, they'd danced above deck to the music floating from the ship's party room. It had been one of those commercially cloying songs she'd always detested, but while in his arms she'd found it to be heartwarming and sweet.

Trying to dislodge the memory, she sought an excuse to refuse. Before she thought of one, Mark caught her wrist and swung her into his arms. "Behave now," he told her. "Your grandma's watching."

"It's you she's worried about, not me," Celie murmured, but she fell into step. Although dancing with him might stir her grandmother's suspicions, refusing his invitation outright would be akin to waving a red flag.

He kept a respectable distance between them as she followed his lead to "The Waltz of the Flowers." Reminding herself it was only a social courtesy she'd accepted, she smiled and said what she'd say to every partner during the evening. "I hope you're enjoying yourself."

"I am now."

Dancing on the ship she'd melted in his arms. She couldn't stop remembering, and the thought made it impossible to relax now. Even in heels, she couldn't see over his shoulder, so she had little choice except to look at his face while they danced. She did her best to disguise her uneasiness by offering him her most brilliant smile.

"So this is how you spend your spare time." Mark eyed her gown with obvious appreciation, his gaze lingering on her shoulders.

"You know how idle we rich really are." She tried not to acknowledge the heat of his hand splayed between her shoulder blades or her reaction to it. It would be best, she knew, to treat him like any other guest, to keep the conversation centered on trivia until the dance ended and she could move on to other partners. She searched for a harmless topic, but the question that had nagged at her since he walked into the ballroom spilled out. "How did you manage it?"

"Ma'am?"

She resisted the boyish grin, even though she allowed him to urge her a millimeter closer. "Spare me the phony drawl, please."

"The drawl is genuine."

"Maybe, but you summon it at will. How did you con Charlie into bringing you here?"

"Con?" An injured look crossed Mark's face. "Charlie and I worked together on an Armed Services committee during Operation Desert Storm. I forgot he lived in Boston until you mentioned his name this morning. Small world, isn't it?"

"Incredibly."

"My grandma believes everything happens for a purpose, and I'm beginning to think she's right. Turns out that Charlie insisted on hitting his favorite watering holes on the way here, and he enlisted me to be his designated driver."

She refused to be diverted by Charlie's drinking habits. "Why didn't you tell me this morning that you knew him?"

"As I recall, you rushed off before we had time to talk about anything."

He spoke as if there were something to be said, as if he knew she still didn't have her reasons for changing her mind down pat, despite a full day's contemplation. Even if she had, this wasn't the time or the place to discuss them. "Did you tell him about us?"

"There's nothing about us to tell." Mark touched one of her earrings. "Very nice. Gift from a previous fiancé?"

His fingertip brushed her earlobe, igniting nerve endings lower in her body. Tilting her head away from his disturbing touch, she tried to decide whether he was joking or jealous. "They came with the family name. Don't admire them too much. Grandmother thinks you're a burglar in disguise, and she might have security escort you through the front gate."

He laughed. "Is that why you've been hovering over me since I walked through the door?"

When his breath stirred her hair, she found it difficult to concentrate on anything. "I wasn't hovering . . ."

"Here I thought you were afraid I'd commit some unspeakable social blunder."

Hurt that he'd consider her in such an unfavorable light, she drew away. "I'm only worried my grandmother will do something foolish."

Gentle pressure from his hand on her back coaxed her close again. "Would it ease her mind if I told her I'm interested in her granddaughter, not the family knickknacks?"

Celie studied his face, unable to hide the alarm skittering over her own. "You wouldn't! You promised."

"I promised," Mark echoed. "All right, your grandmother's off limits. What should I know about your Aunt Louise?"

"Nothing." Celie regretted her hasty response, fearing it could only arouse his suspicion. "She's just as bloodthirsty and vicious as Grandmother."

That wasn't quite true, Celie thought with a twinge of guilt. Her great-aunt trailed in Grandmother's footsteps, soothing ruffled feathers, righting unrighted wrongs. No doubt if Louise took a liking to Mark, she'd fit a broken engagement into the latter category.

"I think she's more like you," Mark said. "Iron backbone, maybe, but soft, like one of those steel magnolias from the South whom I keep hearing about."

He slid his hand down to the small of Celie's back, leaving a trail of white heat beneath her skin as he edged her nearer to him. She didn't resist, even though the way his eyes darkened made her stomach flutter. She should look away, at least focus on his blunt chin or his square jaw. But she didn't, unable to do more than stare into his eyes, aware if she moved another inch toward him they'd be touching thigh-to-thigh.

They slowed to a walk as the music ended. Though it sounded tempting, she refused his request for the next dance. As hostess she had certain responsibilities, but while dancing with him, she'd forgotten the other guests milling around the ballroom.

Making an effort to look busy, she walked to the refreshment table and inspected the ice swan, then straightened a platter of petits fours. She accepted a glass of champagne from a tuxedoed waiter and sipped it while she surveyed the crowd.

Although she told herself she wasn't looking for anyone in particular, she couldn't help but notice Mark whirling around the floor with one of the blond Stewart twins. The subdued light from the chandelier above played over his black hair as he moved with an innate grace even her grandmother would be hard-pressed to criticize.

Trying to observe him with a sense of detachment, Celie noticed she could pick out his laugh over the noise of the crowd and the orchestra combined. She placed her glass on the table and reminded herself she had to attend to the guests.

Moving through the crowd, she listened to long-winded stories of children and grandchildren, nodded her appreciation at compliments regarding the decorations, danced, and dispensed small talk. All the while some internal radar kept her informed of where Mark stood, told her just when he looked across the room and smiled, rankled her when he danced with the women who fawned over his uniform.

By rights he should be out of place, ill at ease, a stranger to her lifestyle. He blended in perfectly. So much for her grandmother's theories on designer genes.

Precisely at eleven o'clock, Grandmother ushered the guests into the anteroom. Celie located her porcelain place card at the head table, Charlie's to her right. A place setting had been squeezed in to the left of hers, with Mark's name scrawled on a makeshift parchment name tag. Since Charlie had found a partner, he and Mark should have been relegated to a guest table. She couldn't help wondering whether Aunt Louise was trying her hand at matchmaking, then immediately reprimanded herself for being so suspicious.

"Thought we'd catch up on old times," Charlie told her. "We should get together for dinner. I'll have my secretary call you and set up something."

Mark spared Celie from refusing. "Charlie says you've known each other since you were six," he said, holding her chair until she sat.

Just how much had Charlie said? Until she knew for certain, she decided to volunteer a minimal amount of information. "He grew up next door."

Charlie didn't notice her reluctance to talk. "Did everything together, didn't we, Celie? Elementary school, college, even law school."

"Then we went our separate ways." She decided to end the story before he could elaborate. "He jumped into politics, and I joined the staff at the Resource Center."

"Such a depressing place." Charlie picked up his wineglass, sampled the contents, then nodded his approval. "I can't believe you're still there, and doing volunteer work, for Pete's sake. When are you going to get a real job?"

"When the center is allocated funds to hire a staff lawyer," she said evenly, turning toward Mark. "Charlie believes people should pull themselves up by their own bootstraps.

"The commander grew up on a dirt farm out west," Charlie interjected. "I'm sure he knows the value of hard work." After emptying his glass in a few swallows, he signaled a waiter for a refill, then changed the subject. "I'm looking for a new press agent, Celie. Why don't you come aboard?"

Press agent? Now she had no doubts as to the reason he'd persuaded Grandmother to give him a seat at the head table, although it shouldn't have surprised her. Everything Charlie did was for his own good. He sat waiting for her answer, and she shook her head. "You know I'm not interested in politics."

"Consider it a favor for an old friend," he urged. "Think about it a few days, give me a call."

"I don't need a few days, Charlie. The answer is no." She posed a question before he could argue the point. "I understand you and the commander worked together?"

Charlie nodded. "Desert Storm. He wanted to be where the action was, but the brass stuck him behind a desk in the Pentagon. Made him mad as—"

"Don't make me sound like a warmonger. Although Mark smiled, his words were cool. "It makes better sense to station officers with combat experience."

Both had plenty more to say, she realized, and she interrupted before tempers flared, steering the conversation toward less volatile topics. They discussed cars over the watercress salad, sports while eating salmon mousse, and movies while feasting on the chocolate-raspberry Sacher torte imported from Austria.

All the while Celie pretended her senses weren't going haywire whenever she looked at Mark. Although decorum dictated she divide her attention equally between her two dinner guests, whenever she looked at Charlie, she thought of Mark.

When the dessert dishes were cleared, Grandmother stepped to the podium set at the end of the head table. The room quieted immediately. With an economy of words, she welcomed her guests, then motioned Celie to the microphone.

She'd learned from Grandmother that a few well-chosen words drew more attention than a long-winded speech. "The purpose behind this ball is to raise money for the less fortunate children of Boston. Let me show you where your dollars will go."

Requesting the overhead lights be dimmed, she proceeded with a slide show she'd designed. Disregarding her usual practice of showing robust children in daycare centers and playgrounds, she'd accompanied a photographer into the darkest sections of the city, searching for haunting scenes people in the room would otherwise never see.

She flicked through the slides to keep shock value at its keenest. A newborn wailing on bare, rusted bedsprings. A toddler dangling a dead rat by its tail. A pre-teen, her body swollen by pregnancy.

When the lights were turned on again, Celie studied the horrified faces before her. "These children are our future. Please be generous."

A standing ovation accompanied her as she walked to her seat. She smiled at the audience before she sat, pleased to see people completing the pledge cards her mother and Aunt Louise were distributing.

"Not so idle after all, are you?" Mark murmured. "No wonder Charlie wants you to join his campaign committee. You could charm the public into voting for anything he proposes."

Glowing at the new respect she saw in his eyes, she reminded herself she wanted him to remember her as he'd known her from the cruise—carefree, a femme fatale without a cause. Just the way Charlie viewed her, as a bored socialite killing time at the center.

She reached for her glass, but instead of drinking, she merely ran her finger around the rim while she absorbed Mark's admiration. "Some things are worth fighting for, Commander," she said softly.

"I know."

Feeling off balance at his slow smile, she searched for something clever to say, anything to drag his attention away from the flush scalding her cheeks. *Stop being so narcissistic,* she scolded herself, knowing he could easily be referring to any of a hundred things other than her.

Charlie clutched her free hand. "Great, Celie, just great."

His words sounded slurred. She noticed that the bottle of champagne he'd earlier convinced the waiter to leave on the table now sat empty.

"Why don't you come back to Washington with me?" Charlie spoke too loudly, attracting attention from several nearby tables. "I have some great ideas—"

"Right now I'd rather you worry about your donation." She flagged a servant carrying a pot of coffee, making certain Charlie's cup was filled before she excused herself from the table. At the anteroom door, she joined her grandmother to personally thank each contributor who'd completed a pledge card.

Last in line, Charlie grimaced as he handed her his card. "The commander convinced me to double my donation," he grumbled good-naturedly. "I'm going to draft him to head my campaign fund committee. How 'bout it, Commander?

He lurched when he turned to look for Mark, who quickly steadied him. "Not interested, Charlie. I had a taste of politics working on that committee with you, and it didn't sit well at all. Too much paperwork just to order a ballpoint pen."

Katherine looped her arm through Charlie's and led him into the hallway. "Let's duck into the kitchen for a cup of coffee," she suggested. "I haven't had a chance to talk with you all night."

"Charlie's had a rough day," Celie said, for the benefit of the lingering guests who'd overheard. She could tell her grandmother wasn't fooled, and she knew that with one target gone, she'd seek out another soon enough. At the moment, Mark appeared the closest victim.

Opening strains of the "Blue Danube" waltz floated from the ballroom. Seizing a perfect opportunity to rescue Mark from becoming Grandmother's prey, Celie turned toward him. "Care to dance, Commander?"

"Perhaps you'll honor me another time," Mark murmured, surprising her. "I've promised this one to a very intriguing lady."

The other blond Stewart twin, no doubt. Jealousy clawed at Celie. Not that it was any of her business if he chose to flirt with every vivacious blonde in the room; after all, his previous fiancées—all five of them—had been blondes. She'd thought that funny when he had told her the first night they'd met, but just thinking about it now made her stomach clench.

"I believe we're finished, Cecilia." Grandmother clutched her arm and indicated she was ready to return to her guests.

Escorting her to the ballroom, Celie paused at a refreshment table. As hostess, she couldn't turn down invitations to dance, yet every time she'd stepped onto the floor, she'd found her attention captured not by her partner, but by Mark. Perhaps if she busied herself, the male guests might ignore her and find more appreciative dance partners.

After getting Grandmother a glass of sherry, Celie chose a chocolate-lace cookie from a silver platter, nibbling it while she surveyed the ballroom. She nearly choked when she spotted Mark whirling her great-aunt around the dance floor.

Grandmother noticed, too. "That old fool," she muttered. "She'll have a heart attack. Where's your mother when I need her?"

She stamped away, her cane clicking against the wood floor. Fighting an impulse to move closer to the dance floor, Celie stayed where she was and tried to lip-read what her great-aunt Louise was saying.

Whatever it was, Louise conducted a one-sided conversation while Mark listened with rapt attention.

In a few moments, Grandmother returned, forcing Celie to drag her attention away from Mark. "Katherine's taken the congressman upstairs to sleep off his whiskey in one of the guest rooms." Grandmother rested both hands on her cane while she watched her sister waltz. "Send that sailor home when this dance is over," she finally ordered. "I'm not about to turn my place into a roadhouse. I'll tell Patrick to have the car waiting."

Celie groaned inwardly, knowing the chauffeur would no doubt report he'd delivered Mark right to Celie's doorstep. She hoped Mark had driven her car; that way he could make an unsupervised getaway.

"It's late; don't bother Patrick. I'll take care of it, Grandmother," Celie said soothingly, inching her grandmother toward a group of bejeweled matrons discussing their most recent trip to Paris.

Before she walked away, Grandmother threw a final scathing glance toward the dance floor. "What in heaven's name can they be talking about?"

Celie wondered the same thing as she straightened a pile of monogrammed napkins. She hoped Louise was recounting her teenage days when she'd eloped with a barnstorming pilot. When prompted, she could talk for hours about anything to anyone.

It took ages for the dance to end. Celie tried to focus her concentration on the crowd in general as Mark escorted Louise to the refreshment table, but she failed miserably.

Her eyes sparkling, Louise fanned her flushed face with a linen napkin before accepting the glass of punch Celie offered. "Thank you, dear," she said. "Are you having a good time?"

"Of course. If you'll excuse me, the commander and I need to—"

"We were just discussing you." Louise took a sip of punch.

Anticipating the worst, Celie squared her shoulders and gritted her teeth into a smile. "You were?"

"Your aunt mentioned your birthday is two days after Christmas," Mark said. "She doesn't know what present to get you."

Trying not to sag with relief, Celie refilled her aunt's emptied glass. "You don't have to get me anything."

"I suggested something for your hope chest," Mark continued. The glint in his eyes warned Celie it was time to put the conversation to rest. "I don't have a hope chest. Commander Edwards, I need to talk—"

Louise clasped Celie's hand. "It's a wonderful idea, isn't it? Your great-grandmother's chest is still in the attic, hand-carved black walnut, I think it is. We could get it refinished. You never know when the right man will come along, do you?"

Celie refused to meet Mark's gaze. "Aunt Louise, I really don't need—"

"We'll discuss it later, dear." Louise patted Celie's arm. "The commander says you promised him this dance."

Mark's eyebrows shot up at Celie's protest. "Surely you aren't going to break *another* promise, Miss Cecilia?"

"I didn't make *another* promise, Commander," Celie reminded him. "Besides, it's nearly midnight."

"Afraid my carriage will turn into a pumpkin?"

She laughed for her great-aunt's sake. "The ball ends officially at midnight, Commander," she pointed out, deciding it best not to mention some guests would linger until dawn. "In case you haven't noticed, Charlie is . . ."

"Drunk?" Mark supplied when she hesitated to search for an acceptable word.

"Indisposed. He's spending the night upstairs." Celie smiled an apology at her aunt. "Excuse us, Louise. I'll walk the commander to his car."

She breathed easier when he bid Louise good-night and offered his arm instead of the objection she'd anticipated.

"Did you check your coat when you came in?" she asked as they walked out of the ballroom.

"My coat's here; your car isn't. I left it at your place and drove Charlie's instead. But no problem; I'll call a cab."

She directed him to the closest phone, one in the cavernous front hall. Mark glanced at the grand staircase as they walked past it, and stopped to admire the gilt-framed ancestral portraits lining the entrance hallway walls. "Puts some of the homes I've seen in Europe to shame," he said. "What was it your ancestors did, anyhow?"

Leafing through the phone book, Celie found a number for a cab company before she answered. "They stockpiled guns before the Revolutionary War started, cotton before the Civil War. Grandmother shocked Wall Street by investing heavily in computers when they were just playthings."

"Quite a lady, your Aunt Louise," he said after he'd called for a cab. "She says she's ridden the wings of a bi-plane so many times she's lost count."

If Louise relayed her detailed teenage adventures, she wouldn't have had time to talk of anything else. That thought made Celie breathe easier as she accompanied Mark to the coat-check closet outside the ballroom to retrieve his coat.

He shook his head when he realized she intended to follow him, through the front door. "Beautiful as that gown is, it's not covering enough of you to be worn outside. I'm certain the cab will be here in no time."

Besides needing a breath of fresh air to clear her senses, she wanted to see the cab drive away. Until Mark was safely out of sight, she couldn't give her guests the attention they deserved.

She casually dismissed his concern, then wished she hadn't seconds later as she stepped from the enclosed front porch into the frosty night. Her teeth chattered too much to make even a token protest when he shrugged off his coat and draped it around her shoulders.

He fastened the top button, then slid his hand over her neck to tame her hair whipping in the wind. "This is winter weather I like," he said, his words making translucent puffs in the air. "Look up."

The ominous clouds had rolled on, leaving in their wake an indigo sky glittering with stars. "Beautiful," she whispered, although all she could think about was his breath warming her temple.

She knew he wanted to kiss her. She wanted him to kiss her until she was lost, unable to think, with only her senses to guide her. Blinded by emotion, the way she'd been aboard the ship.

The thought sobered her. Tilting her head to pull her hair free from his grasp, she stepped away. "You can meet the cab at the front gate. Good night."

She turned too quickly back to the house, causing her narrow heels to skid over an icy patch on the brick walk.

Mark caught her. "Slow down before you break your neck."

"I've survived thirty Boston winters on my own," she reminded him, although she didn't pull away.

"You haven't built up an immunity yet." His hands tunneled under the coat to warm her arms. "Look, you're shivering. Go back inside."

A very sensible suggestion. She knew it was time to pull away, to shrug off his coat and return it, but she found she couldn't do anything except wish for the moment to last. The reflection of the yard lights off the fresh snow combined with the music filtering from the ballroom lent an intimacy to the night that sent her pulse jackhammering. "I'm fine," she whispered.

Except that she wasn't fine at all. Rather than returning to a room filled with people she barely knew, she wanted to be alone with Mark. She heard her breath falter when he brushed his thumbs over her collarbones.

His lips touched her temple, heating her skin. "Come home with me."

She felt the lure, as strong now as it had been aboard ship, urging her to cast aside her obligations and run into the future, savoring, anticipating, trusting fate would tie up the loose ends.

And she knew once again she'd wake up tomorrow, terrified she'd made a mistake. She hadn't yet recovered from the last one. She stared at his face shadowed by the near dark. "I can't."

"Right." He drew a deep breath, exhaled, and tucked his hands in his pockets. "I can't begin to offer you what Charlie could."

She almost laughed at the underlying resentment in his words. "Charlie can't offer me anything. He stopped trying years ago."

"He told me you two were engaged."

She should have guessed Charlie would have played that bit of trivia for whatever is was worth. "We were. Our mothers pushed us together when we were eighteen."

"What happened?"

After the initial thrill had faded, she had realized marriage meant she and Charlie would spend the next fifty years side by side. She'd found the possibility depressing. "Grandmother insisted I was too young to know what I wanted."

"Bless her stony little heart," Mark murmured. She felt the tension running through him dissipate. He touched her cheek, then skimmed her hair with his fingers. "You're old enough now. What do you want?"

To close the distance between them and lose herself in his warmth, to let him make utter chaos of her dwindling common sense. She'd never felt so vulnerable before, and the feeling confused her. "I'm old enough to know there's a difference between what people want and what they need."

He waved at the cab pulling in front of the massive iron gate. "Sometimes it's one and the same."

"Rarely. It's getting late." The reminder was more for her sake than his, because he made no move to approach the cab.

"Almost midnight." With his thumb he traced her upper lip. "The bewitching hour."

She couldn't move and, for a moment, couldn't breathe. Lowering his head, he brushed her lips with his own, sending a burst of pleasure through her. Dangerous as it was, she wanted more. Or needed more. For the moment, she couldn't distinguish between the two.

Nor could she stand feeling this way, disoriented and heady, more than willing to plunge into the unknown. What she wanted most to do was shut her eyes and listen to her heart. An appalling idea; trusting base instinct had led her into trouble in the first place.

Besides, she had no wish to be his ex-fiancée number six, left behind to cry and want long after he was gone. It wouldn't matter who called it quits; somewhere along the way passion would fade, replaced by a void that neither could fill. She wasn't fool enough to think a few happy memories would quell the pain.

Steeling her self-determination, she unbuttoned Mark's coat and slipped it off her shoulders. "Good night, Mark," she said, handing it to him. "I need to get back to my guests."

He let the coat fall to the ground as he cupped her bare shoulders with his hands. "Take this back inside with you."

His lips barely touching hers, he gave her a butterfly kiss. His tongue flitted across her lips, teasing them apart.

Move away, her mind warned. Move she did, but farther into his embrace, relaxing her mouth, inviting the kiss to deepen. Shrouded by the shadows, she snuggled against his muscled heat, taking all the time she needed to savor the taste and feel of him, shivering no longer from cold but from the need spiraling unchecked from her head to her toes.

Mark stepped away first, his hands lingering to soothe her tousled hair. "I don't want to overstay my welcome," he whispered hoarsely, scooping up his coat. He strode to the waiting cab before she managed to say anything.

Five

Mark cursed himself all the way home. Stupid trick, wrangling an invitation to the city's slickest ball. Even more foolish, he had thought if he kissed Celie senseless, he might change her mind.

Small comfort she expressed no interest in Charlie. He'd seen at least a dozen wealthier, more powerful men dancing with her tonight, corporate titans complete with lineage and legacies.

Inside Celie's house, he stood in the living room. Alone, he could still smell her perfume, hear her laugh, taste her. With one kiss he'd blown away his best intentions to keep his distance until he'd proved something far deeper than hormones drew them together. He'd probably lost every inch of ground he'd gained to date.

Then again, she'd kissed him back.

The spark existed, waiting to be fanned into fire. It was inevitable. They belonged together, with a need that went far deeper than passion. On the ship, he had known his fate had been decided the moment he'd seen her. Now he needed to curb his impatience, step back, and let her realize what he'd discovered—it wasn't a conscious decision for them—for him or for her—to make. After all, fate decreed they belonged together, right as rain.

Of course, he had the advantage. His grandmother had preached predestiny since his cradle days, telling him he'd know without a doubt when his woman walked into his life. A few times he'd mistaken a surge of attraction for that undeniable sign, only to discover mere attraction waned fast.

Not this time. Fate had dropped Celie into his arms; it was up to him to keep her there.

Tonight he needed to set things right. The moment Celie walked in the door, he'd confess he'd received the lettergram. Together they could work through her fears, peeling them away one at a time until she felt ready to embrace her fate.

* * *

His legs were cramped.

Mark stretched, then, when his feet hit the end of the sofa, realized he wasn't in bed. Sitting, he tried to rub a kink out of his neck while he figured out what had awakened him.

Illuminated by the light from the television, Celie sat across the room while she played messages from her answering machine. Glancing at his watch, he saw it was nearly four in the morning. A sound sleeper, he hadn't heard her come in.

He stretched his arms over his head while he watched her dial a number, then listened to the soothing apology she offered to someone she'd awakened on the other end of the line. It wasn't polite to eavesdrop, he reminded himself, and busied himself by searching for his shoes.

The sudden anger infusing her words made him look up. Her voice was still quiet and steady, but there was no mistaking the fire behind it. He'd hate to be on the receiving end; however, he couldn't help envying whatever inspired it. Apparently she was willing to fight to the end for some things. He wished he were one of them.

After replacing the receiver, she picked up her purse and walked halfway across the room before she noticed he was watching her. She offered a distracted smile. "Sorry I woke you. Where are my car keys?"

He scooped them off the coffee table, then frowned and checked his watch again. "You aren't going out now?"

"There's a battered child waiting in the emergency room, and I'm on call tonight—" She shook her head as he stood and grabbed his coat draped over a nearby wing chair. "Mark, there's no reason for you to come."

"There are plenty of reasons, the first being I'll never get back to sleep knowing you're skidding around the streets of Boston at four in the morning."

Although Celie worked with ruthless efficiency to complete myriad forms, it was after dawn before she delivered the two-year-old to the custody of a foster parent.

Outside the hospital, as he pulled from the plowed parking lot, Mark glanced at Celie. She hadn't spoken since they'd left the emergency room, merely handing him the keys and climbing into the passenger seat. Her eyes were closed, but he knew by her uneven breathing that she wasn't asleep.

He imagined one would build up an immunity to such horrors in her line of work, but she appeared shaken and pale. "I guess you don't do this often," he said.

For several moments, she didn't answer. When she did, her voice shook. "It never gets easier, if that's what you're asking. I thought the longer I worked, the less susceptible I'd be. I guess I am, in a way. The first time I had to deal with a battered child I spent half the time crying in the restroom."

In the dim light afforded by the streetlamps, he studied her rigid posture. "You probably felt better afterward."

"It didn't help at all." Horrified to feel tears burning behind her eyes, she turned to stare out the passenger window. She hadn't cried in public since her father's funeral; her grandmother simply did not permit it. Now she couldn't help herself. She brushed away the tears as fast as they slid over her cheeks until her hands were wet. Letting her hair curtain her face, she dug through her purse for a tissue.

The car stopped. A traffic light, she supposed, surprised when she heard Mark switch off the ignition. They hadn't traveled far enough to be home yet, but she didn't trust her voice enough to ask where they were.

She felt him push the hair from her face. She tried to turn back toward the window, but he caught her chin, forcing her to face him. "It's all right to cry," he said.

"Not in my family, it isn't." She couldn't stop the sobs tearing from her throat.

Muttering something unkind about her family, Mark hauled her across the seat until she rested next to him. When she tried to pull away, he wrapped his arms around her, stroking her hair and murmuring encouragements until she relaxed against his chest.

She didn't know how long she cried, only that she would feel humiliated when she finally finished. But once he started the engine, she found herself too exhausted to experience any emotion, too weary to crawl back into the other seat where she belonged.

Still holding her, he freed the emergency brake and manipulated the gearshift. "Do you want to stop somewhere for breakfast?"

"I'm not hungry." Nor was she ready to face the world red-eyed and sniffling. She'd already blown her chance to show him just how cool and controlled she always was. "I'm sorry I fell apart."

His arm tightened. "Stop talking like you cried over a broken fingernail."

"It just seems so unfair. That little girl should be waking up this week to a pile of Christmas gifts, not multiple bruises and contusions." She fished another tissue from her purse and blew her nose. "I never cry."

"What do you do?"

"Work with a social worker to find foster care, document physical signs of abuse, gather evidence to obtain a warrant—"

"That's not what I meant. What do you do instead of crying?"

"I try harder." She drew a deep breath to keep her voice steady, businesslike. "Fight for more state and federal funding for family-counseling centers. Ours is a prototype funded by several area corporations in the area.

"I mean, what do you do for *yourself?*"

"I don't need anything for myself," she said, irritated that he'd think she did.

"You can't solve all this city's problems, and you're only going to burn yourself out trying."

Her chin jutted out. "It's what I want to do."

He eased the car to a stop at the red light. "I don't know about that. I think you have all this empty space in your life and you're desperate to fill it with something worthwhile. Right now the only thing you have is your job. Maybe you need to balance that with other interests."

She didn't appreciate hearing from him what Shannon and Vera had been saying for years. "You, I suppose?"

"Why not?"

When she turned her head to tell him why, he kissed her, his hands cradling her head, his thumbs rubbing the last traces of tears from her cheeks.

Behind them, a car honked.

When he let her go, she scrambled back to her side of the car. Try as she might, all the way home she couldn't forget the feel of his mouth on hers, promising, possessive, sweet, and for the moment, filling the void in her life.

When Celie came downstairs, she found Mark sprawled on the sofa. He looked up from the Sunday newspaper spread around him and smiled at her. "Get enough sleep?"

Celie nodded. It had been years since she'd slept until noon. Then again, it had been years since she'd arrived home so tired she could barely climb the stairs.

He appeared none the worse for the wear. Clean-shaven, bright-eyed, teeming with energy, he looked the way she'd first seen him above deck waiting for the apricot-streaked Caribbean dawn to appear.

"What are we going to do today?" He interrupted the memory, reminding her those days had passed.

"*I* have work to do."

"It's Sunday."

It was, but she felt that if she could get her daily routine back to normal, the rest of her life might follow suit. "I always catch up on my paperwork on Sunday."

"What day don't you do anything?"

"Waste time?" She felt herself recoil at the idea, years of her grandmother's ingrained discipline kicking into gear. "There's always something to do."

"All right." He retrieved the comic section and settled back against the cushions. "I hoped you'd help me finish my Christmas shopping, but if you intend to ruin your Sunday shut inside this house, I'll do the same."

He'd opened the drapes to the bay window, and outside she could see the midday sunlight sparkling against the snow. Perfect day for a winter's walk, she realized, feeling her best intentions waver.

"Just for a few hours," he coaxed. "Help me pick out some Christmas things. Not much, just a couple ornaments, maybe a string of lights. We had some on the sub that played electronic carols."

She tried not to cringe at the idea of a microchip chirping "Silent Night."

"Tacky, I know. I looked through your CDs—didn't see any Christmas music. We'll pick up a few today."

"I don't need any. Decorations, either." She didn't want him handling her belongings, becoming familiar with her life. Keeping her world to herself had helped make breaks in the past less painful. "Shannon flies to Nassau every year, and I spend Christmas Day at my family's."

She busied herself refolding the scattered sections of the paper. He stilled her hands, waiting until she looked at him before he spoke. "Christmas is a season, not a day. Technically speaking, there are twelve days of Christmas, and most people spend them *with* their families. Doesn't matter where Shannon goes—you need to haul out the holly for yourself."

He couldn't possibly know what she needed. Lately she couldn't even decide herself. She tried to shake away his fingers circling her wrist, but he held fast.

"Remember, we aren't going to spend every Christmas with your family," he said, his voice softening. "Once we have children we'll need to establish some traditions of our own."

She needed more sleep; otherwise, her mind wouldn't have painted a picture of sailor-suited toddlers toppling a stack of presents. "We aren't *establishing* anything."

Instead of arguing, he changed the subject. "Have you finished your Christmas shopping?"

Since her lack of decorations bothered him, she could imagine how he'd react to her perspective toward gifts. Not that it mattered what he thought, she reminded herself. "I don't give presents."

"Not even to your family?"

"Christmas isn't something the Hargraves celebrate in the traditional way."

"Why not?"

How could she explain to someone who'd been born into a *real* family? No doubt a mother who mailed home-baked cookies also doled out hugs and kisses along with the Christmas gifts. "If there's something we want or need, we buy it. That makes gift giving rather pointless."

Pulling on her boots, hat, coat, and mittens kept her occupied and gave her an excuse to avoid his thoughtful scrutiny.

Outside, Mark offered his arm to escort her down the steps. "Want me to drive?"

"It would take us longer to find a parking space than it would to walk," she pointed out, leading the way.

She always walked briskly with a goal in mind, but today with Mark at her side, she found that impossible. He paused every few steps to pack snowballs, which he tossed against the wrought-iron fences guarding the tiny yards along the street.

She checked her watch when they stopped a fourth time. Alone she could cover a mile in fifteen minutes; in that time today, they hadn't yet walked three blocks. She started to tell him so, but he pushed back her coat sleeve, unclasped the watch, and dropped it into his pocket.

"I never thought I'd be jealous of an inanimate object," he grumbled. "You've given that watch all your attention since we left your house. I just hit a bull's eye and you didn't even notice. Put years of expertise into that shot thinking you'd reward me, and what do I get?"

"I let you have my watch, didn't I?" As she spoke his gaze dropped to her mouth. Even through layers of down and wool, she could feel her body reacting, the unwanted attraction her mind had battled against since she had come downstairs that morning flaring to life. Still, this time she was prepared, and she steeled herself, determined to make the kiss cool and unresponsive.

He only brushed a strand of hair off her cheek. "It must have been great growing up here."

Her heart tumbled crazily for a moment after he withdrew his fingers. Disappointment, she assured herself, because she hadn't been allowed to prove herself immune, not pure regret that he hadn't kissed her after all. "I never played outside in the winter when I was growing up."

"Come on. Didn't your mother take you sledding or ice-skating?"

The thought of Katherine in her tailored silk dress and pearls twirling around a frozen pond made Celie laugh. "She'd eat nails first. Hargraves like inside sports like backgammon or bridge."

Mark shook his head. "I thought everyone in New England spent their free time skiing."

"Shannon does."

"So do I. We'll drive somewhere tomorrow and I'll show you the ropes."

"Maybe." Her polite response served as a definite refusal.

"Chicken?"

She refused to rise to his good-natured taunt. "I have enough hobbies, thank you."

"Where's your sense of adventure?"

"People in my family are born without one."

Mark chuckled. "Then your Aunt Louise must be a changeling, I suppose, eloping and performing with a bi-plane pilot?"

"Did she mention she was widowed three weeks later when his plane crashed into a telegraph pole? She's lucky she was on the ground at the time."

"She's lucky she had those few weeks of fun to spark up her otherwise mundane life. She told me that herself."

Celie couldn't help wondering what had precipitated the conversation but decided it was better not to know. "Some of us are content leaving our mundane lives exactly the way they are."

Although she expected an argument, he just smiled and handed her a snowball he'd made. "Hold this a moment."

He piled six more in her arms before he reclaimed them all. Suddenly wary of the wicked glint in his eyes, Celie frowned. "I'm too old to play games."

His smile broadened as he backed away.

"Mark, *you're* too old to play games." Even Grandmother Grace's perfectly mimicked tones failed to thwart him.

A snowball plopped against her shoulder and shattered into chunky powder over the front of her jacket. She ducked when he aimed again, and managed to bat the second one away. "Stop," she ordered, knowing the laughter infusing her command made it ineffectual.

When he lifted his arm to toss a third, she stooped and packed a ball of her own. "You'd better stop," she warned.

"Or what?"

"Or I'll—"

After dodging another one he pitched, she stood and hurled hers. It struck him in the forehead. Clasping a hand over his eyes, he stumbled, then fell face first into a snowbank.

"Mark?" Alarmed when he didn't respond, she ran and knelt by his side. Tugging off her mittens she raked her fingers through his hair, searching his scalp for blood. Her pulse pounded against her temples when he remained motionless.

Without warning, he rolled over, caught her shoulders, and pulled her close. She could hear laughter rumbling in his chest as she struggled to escape his hold.

"Of all the despicable—"

His kiss warmed her lips, heated her blood, and she could think of nothing else but how hungry her mouth was against his.

Finally he lifted his head and rolled her over, his weight pinning her into the snow. "Uncle?"

She fought an impulse to pull his face down to hers, instead wiping her mouth with the back of her hand. "Uncle, my eye."

"Close enough." He stood and offered his hand to help her to her feet. Laughing, he brushed the snow from his coat and hers. "Saw that once in a movie. Always wondered whether it really worked."

Celie found her mittens and jerked them on. "It won't work next time."

"Next time?"

Refusing to be caught in his playful mood, she marched ahead, her boots crunching against the packed snow on the sidewalk. There was a certain saneness in dating predictable men. She couldn't name one who'd act like a child and instigate a snowball battle. And Mark collapsing in the snow and faking an injury—such a juvenile trick, she couldn't believe she'd been gullible enough to be deceived.

A smile tugged at the corner of her lips the more she thought about it, and before she could suppress it, he'd caught up with her.

"You should do that more often," he said. "My grandma says laughing bares the soul."

She stopped short. "Has it occurred to you I don't want my soul bared?"

Righting her hat, he tucked her arm in the crook of his elbow. "When you do want it and I'm gone, who'll be there to listen?"

"Shannon."

Mark shook his head. "Not the same at all. You need someone who'll dream when you dream, cry, when you cry, laugh when you laugh. A soul mate."

"You, I suppose?"

He nodded. "You only have one in the world. If you're mine, I must be yours."

" 'You were meant for me; I was meant for you.' Isn't that a bit simplistic?"

"Preordained by fate. You can protest and drag your heels all you want, but in the end, you'll be mine."

She had a troubled feeling he really believed what he said. "I don't put much faith in fate."

"No, I imagine you live by the Puritan work ethic. Work hard, obey the rules, take whatever crumbs fall your way."

"Life's not quite that simple," she pointed out.

"It's as simple as you make it. You can clutter it with dating rituals and pretend you've made an intelligent and rational choice, or you can follow your heart."

He stopped to admire a lopsided snowman. "We should build one of those when we get home. Speaking of dating rituals, you don't need to buy me a Christmas present."

She surprised herself by laughing. "We weren't speaking of dating rituals, and I didn't buy you anything."

"Good. Just being here is the best gift I've ever had. Even better than the horse my grandfather gave me when I was seven. You ever had a horse?"

"A quarter horse." She regretted her flat reply when she realized it might sound condescending. If it did, he didn't seem to notice.

"What did you name it?"

"Thoroughbreds come with names attached." Actually, she'd forgotten, though through no fault of its own. A beautiful horse, it performed well, but meant nothing more to her than allocating endless hours to haute école lessons. To Grandmother's disappointment, she hadn't won a single trophy.

"I called mine Spot," he said, interrupting the memory.

They negotiated an icy section of sidewalk. "Spot is a dog's name."

"My dad called him Mutt because he was a mixed breed. Crazy colored—tan and brown spots all over. I thought Spot sounded a little more dignified."

"A little." Knowing it would be wiser not to hear more about his father or his horse or anything else in his past that stirred her envy, she motioned for them to cross the street.

Around the corner, the residential brownstones were replaced by shops.

"Almost there," she told Mark when he rubbed his reddened hands together. It had been a mistake to walk. The sunshine had made the day look deceptively warm, but even well-bundled as she was, she felt chilled. "You should have worn gloves," she chided. "Do you want to step inside one of these places and get warm?"

He studied a menu taped to the window of a streetside café. "Hot chocolate sounds great."

Inside, she blinked, letting her eyes adjust to the lighting while Mark scanned the tables crowding the floor. "None empty," he said. "Guess we'll have to sit at the counter."

The few available stools weren't side by side. "We could try another place," Celie suggested, before she realized he no longer stood at her side. Around her, customers shifted, sliding off stools and carrying their meals to new locations. In a moment, Mark straddled the end stool and motioned her to the empty one next to his.

"You're too old to play musical chairs," she scolded, although she appreciated his efforts. She unzipped her coat and pulled off her hat.

"I told them I intended to propose."

Her hands froze in midair. Apparently he wasn't joking; all around her, customers were watching, waiting. The restaurant buzzed as word spread from table to table.

She draped her coat on the stool before she sat. "What are you going to tell them when I refuse?" she whispered.

"Why would you?" Mark looked at the chalkboard menu of specials posted behind the counter, then asked the hovering waitress, "What's your house specialty?"

"The chili ain't half bad," she said.

"We'll take two. Wouldn't have any Dom Perignon in stock, would you?" Mark sighed when she shook her head. "Two hot chocolates, then."

Celie waited until the waitress walked away before she spoke. "I can't eat before an audience, Mark."

After glancing at the expectant faces around him, he slid from his stool, knelt on one knee, and took her hands in his. "Will you be mine, Celie? I'll promise you my heart and soul, the sun and the moon, a dishwasher—"

"Get up," she said, trying not to laugh at his earnest expression. "You already know my answer."

Kissing her hands, Mark stood and faced his audience. "The answer's yes, folks," he announced before taking his seat.

"I didn't say—"

"You don't have to. It's in the stars." Mark pulled a handful of napkins from the dispenser and polished the counter in front of him. "I apologize for the unromantic atmosphere. I usually take my women somewhere special for a first date."

"This is not a date, and I am not your woman." She told herself her stomach ached from hunger, not jealousy. Some woman, somewhere, someday, would be very lucky to accept his offer of marriage. It just wouldn't be her.

"You can ask me about them, if you want."

On the cruise, he'd told her they were consistently blond, leggy, athletic, and vivacious. Alike as peas in a pod, all the things she wasn't, which only confounded her more, and proved she definitely wasn't his type. Unfolding a paper napkin, Celie placed it on her lap. "I'm not interested in your past," she lied.

"I'm curious about yours. Louise says after you broke your engagement with the congressman, you met someone else. A doctor."

"A pre-med student." Celie reluctantly made the correction. She wondered whether Aunt Louise had spared Mark the sordid details.

Mark waited for the waitress to place bowls of chili and a basket of soda crackers on the counter before he continued. "What happened?"

"Derrick and I went our separate ways." She saw no need to point out he'd left immediately after discovering her trust fund wouldn't be accessible until she turned thirty. Eleven years, he'd told her, would be too long for him to wait.

"Then there was that Spanish shipping magnate—"

"Jorgé," she supplied, unwilling to offer more. "Louise managed to feed you all this information during one dance?"

"I'm a good listener. That time you'd even planned the wedding, she said."

What *hadn't* Louise told him? Celie sipped her ice water while she considered what to explain about Jorgé. "He swept me off my feet. Once I touched ground, I realized there wasn't much holding our relationship together." Especially after she learned he kept a mistress in Spain and had no intentions of letting a wedding dissolve what he considered a satisfactory arrangement.

"And the CEO?"

Craig's only fault had been catching her on the rebound. Handsome, a former professional golfer, polite to a fault, a lover of poetry and children, he'd have been a model husband. Except, for some inane reason, that just hadn't been enough. How could she explain that to Mark when she couldn't rationalize it herself?

"I think we've probed my past long enough." She hoped her voice indicated the subject was closed.

Mark sampled his chili, then reached for the pepper shaker. "Here I thought I could stir a little interest by leaking our engagement to the press, but they'd probably yawn and toss the story into the nearest trash can."

"I don't know why you sound so surprised." She hated the defensive note crawling into her words. "You've been engaged more than once yourself."

"And I admitted that the first night we met. I should have been suspicious when you didn't recoil with shock."

She bit back a dozen questions about the women he'd loved, knowing in all fairness she'd then owe answers to any questions he'd ask. "Your past is your own business, just as mine is mine. Besides, I would have told you about the others before our wedding, if there had been a wedding."

He concentrated on his chili, finishing it before he pushed away the dish and spoke again. "How many all together?"

Struggling to look confused by the question, although she knew exactly what he meant, Celie frowned. "How many what?"

"Ex-fiancés."

She returned the earthenware cup of hot chocolate to the chipped saucer. "I don't put notches on my belt."

"Estimate."

It irked her that he'd think there were so many men drifting in and out of her life she wouldn't be able to keep track. Still, she provided the answer unwillingly. "Four."

He grinned. "Counting me?"

"Five." She reached for the bill the waitress slapped onto the counter, but Mark got it first.

"Old-fashioned as it sounds, I insist on paying the bill. These engagements—were they all dissolved by mutual agreement?"

Standing, Celie picked up her coat and followed Mark to the cash register. "What difference does it make?"

"I'm curious. Did you leave a string of broken hearts around the city?"

"Amicable partings, every one." She didn't feel it necessary to add that in every case she'd been satisfied with her rational decisions, all made without this mope-around-cry-into-your-pillow nonsense.

He paid the bill and pocketed the change after leaving a tip. "You certainly did the right thing, since they didn't feel you were worth fighting for."

"Maybe I wasn't," she muttered. In each instance, she could have worked to smooth the rough spots. Married Charlie, but lived a life of her own. Provided the money to cover medical-school tuition in the hope true love would follow. Insisted the courtesan go. Resigned herself to a languid life of golf and Keats.

Yet, looking back, she knew without regret she'd made the right decision each time. She'd walked away without lasting regrets, satisfied that severing ties had been the best choice for all concerned. If she could just remember that when the time came for Mark to fly back to Florida, she could keep their parting impersonal.

Six

The enclosed shopping center swarmed with last-minute shoppers. Finding the artificial heat uncomfortable, Celie pulled off her hat and gloves and tucked them in her pocket. "Where to?" she asked, leading Mark to the glass directory in the center of the mall.

He insisted on bypassing the stores and headed for a crafts fair located near the food court.

Stopping at the first table there, Celie examined an ostrich eggshell, one side painstakingly cut away. Inside, a ceramic boy in red pajamas straddling a banister headed toward a Christmas tree at the foot of the stairs.

Mark spoke over her shoulder. "That's what our son will look like—your red hair, freckles, green eyes."

Not wanting him to know she'd been thinking the same thing, she handed the egg to him. "My hair is auburn, my eyes are hazel," she corrected him. "And we aren't having a son."

The clerk tending the table overheard. "You can never be too sure," she said. "At my daughter's sonogram her doctor swore she was carrying a girl. Baby turned out to be a boy, plain as day."

She stole a glance at Celie's waist as she offered her another ornament. "You aren't showing yet. When's your due date?"

Celie elbowed Mark, cutting short his chuckle. "I'm not pregnant."

"Yet," Mark murmured. Ignoring her glare, he inspected the eggshell she held, identical to the first except with a pigtailed girl riding the railing.

"Your grandma's house has that huge staircase," he said. "Ever slide down the banister?"

"Just once." The memory rushed back, vivid as the day it happened twenty-one years ago. "Grandmother met me at the bottom and sentenced me to sit on the landing the rest of the afternoon. Then I had to scrub the lemon oil from my dress with a toothbrush."

She tried to laugh to prove it didn't really matter, but she knew by his frown that he wasn't fooled. "Didn't she have a childhood?"

"Probably not. She had a nanny, Miss Pierce, who also reared my mother. I'm lucky Miss Pierce moved to the Cedar Hills Rest Home before I could benefit from her iron hand." With one last glance at the ornament, Celie tried to return it to the table, but he stopped her.

He handed his charge card to the clerk. "We'll take both."

After writing a receipt, the clerk swathed the ornaments in foam padding and tucked them into a box. "You two keep trying," she gushed as she gave it to Celie. "It took my daughter four years to get pregnant first time around."

Celie thanked her with a stiff smile, then hurried from the booth.

"You look tense," Mark murmured, a thread of laughter running through his voice. "When we get home, I'd be happy to give you a massage."

"You might not live that long," she said, handing him the box. "Don't do that again."

"Do what?"

She couldn't tell what bothered her more, his stirring alive old memories, or his pretending they were ready to start new ones. "Whatever you did back there to make that woman think we were married."

"I didn't say a word about our being married. Maybe we just make the perfect couple. Wait, I want to look at these." Grasping her hand, he pulled her toward a display of cornhusk dolls.

"Wedding angels," the vendor explained when Celie picked up one sporting pink gossamer wings. "They come in pairs."

He handed her another with wings dyed a dark blue, and showed her how to fit them together so their wings interlocked and blended colors, changing to a rich purple. "Personalized free of charge," he added.

"We'll take the set," Mark said. He leaned across the table and lowered his voice. "We aren't married, you know."

Celie ignored his I-did-what-you-told-me grin. Whenever she could, she ordered from a catalog, viewing shopping as a chore to be handled with a minimum of effort. Obviously Mark intended to lurk at each table, inspect everything that caught his eye, and try to drag her not only into the Christmas spirit, but remind her every inch of the way that she'd reneged on a witless promise she'd made.

"I'm going home," she told him. "It's obvious you don't need my help shopping."

Pirates had life easy, he thought, watching her thread her way through the shoppers. See a woman you wanted, drag her back to your ship, she's yours. Not that he'd resort to such barbaric measures. Today's relationships were based on mutual trust and understanding, or at least they should be. With a pang of guilt, he vowed to set things right the moment they returned to her house. He'd admit he'd received the lettergram, rely on fate to turn the tide his way, and start his pursuit anew.

He saw her stop a moment. *Coming back?* He held his breath, releasing it slowly when she turned and walked into a store. He read the brightly lit sign over the doorway: TOY BAZAAR.

"Sir?" The vendor held an angel, his metallic pen posed, at the base. "If you'll just tell me what names . . ."

Mark pulled his wallet from his pocket. "Just wrap them."

He kept his gaze trained on the store's entrance and, after collecting his purchase, hurried to find her.

She stood in the doll aisle, her back to him. Resisting an impulse to cradle her in his arms, he tapped her shoulder. "I'm sorry if I embarrassed you," he said softly. "Sometimes I speak before I think."

Startled, she jumped and spun around. "Apology accepted."

Not expecting the smile she offered, he jammed his hands in his pockets to keep from touching her and ruining his best intentions. He eyed the baby doll she held. "Adding to Shannon's collection?"

"I thought I'd pick up something for that little girl I placed this morning."

He saw dozens of prettier ones on the shelf. "It's sort of plain, isn't it?"

She looked at the painted face as if she hadn't noticed. "It's soft and floppy, one she can cuddle. We aren't supposed to get involved with clients, but I'd hate to have her think Santa's forgotten her."

The wistfulness in her voice surprised him. Tonight, he promised himself, after showing her the lettergram, he'd tackle her lack of Christmas spirit. Apparently, somewhere along the way, Santa had deserted her, and he vowed to make it his personal quest to right that wrong.

It was the most he could offer. No doubt her former fiancés—the thought made his gut tighten—had showered her with jewelry worth more than the salary he pulled in a single year. Not that he could blame them; he'd have done the same thing in their shoes.

No, he'd have done more. Much more.

He couldn't imagine anyone letting her just walk away. Amicable partings, she'd said. If she thought *he'd* settle for such a lukewarm conclusion to the week they'd shared, she was in for a big surprise.

He'd make a point to invite them all to the wedding—Jorgé, the doctor, Charlie, the CEO—just to prove there were no hard feelings. In fact, he'd lift a toast to their honor and thank them for realizing they weren't right for her.

But first he'd have to clear up the little matter of the lettergram.

He waited at her side while she purchased the doll and made arrangements to have it delivered the next day, compliments of "Santa." The act boosted her spirits; he could tell by the way her eyes sparkled, but he knew better than to compliment her for her impulse. No doubt she'd been bred to regard impulsiveness as a weakness.

Old habits were hard to break, but he figured he'd have fun trying. When she'd finished, he took her arm. "Next stop, Music Metropolis."

She halfheartedly protested as they headed for the store. Inside, she followed him to a towering Christmas display and watched him choose a handful of compact disks.

"We'll start with five," he said, showing her his selections. "Bing Crosby, the Mormon Tabernacle Choir, Mantovani, Barbra Streisand, Randy Travis. Christmas background music for later, when we're drinking eggnog in front of your fireplace."

Before she could protest, he steered her toward the counter.

In line, she turned to face him. "We aren't going to—"

"I checked your liquor cabinet. You don't have any rum, although I suppose we could spike eggnog with the Courvoisier."

"It's Shannon's." They stepped forward as the line of customers moved toward the cash register. "I've already lent you her bed. I'm not about to turn over her cognac. And while you're at it, forget about the eggnog and the fireplace."

"I can't. They're a vital part of the dating rituals we were talking about earlier."

"We weren't talking about dating rituals." She had more to say, he could tell, but she clamped her mouth shut when she realized their argument had snared the interest of the other customers waiting in line.

Outside the store, he didn't give her a chance to revive her protests. "You haven't offered any suggestions for your Christmas gift," he pointed out. "At least give me a hint."

"I don't want anything." She tried to pull him toward the exit doors.

"Everyone wants something."

"I have everything I need."

"Except me.

She stopped so suddenly that a woman walking behind collided with her. After apologizing, Celie turned back to Mark. "I don't need you."

He shrugged, certain she was trying to convince herself of that fact, not him. After all, he knew better. "Sooner or later you're going to accept your fate."

"Sooner or later you're going to accept my refusal."

Forget the fireplace. He could spend the day standing in the middle of Christmas mayhem just watching her fight a smile.

She touched her hair. "I'd appreciate it if you didn't look at me like that," she said uneasily.

"Like what?"

"Like you're—"

He grinned, waiting while she searched for the word she wanted. "Smitten."

"I am."

She didn't pursue the issue. "Are you finished shopping?"

Praying for inspiration, Mark studied the storefronts around him. What could he buy a woman who had everything? "I haven't bought your present," he reminded her.

"Then we're even, because I don't have anything for you, either. Let's go."

Relieved when he didn't protest, she led the way to the plate-glass exit doors. Stepping outside felt like walking into a block of ice. She zipped her jacket to her chin and tugged on her hat, shivering too much to object when Mark flagged a cab.

"I ought to send your grandmother something for letting me into the ball," he said, as he opened the cab door. "Maybe a bottle of fine wine?"

"Gifts from strangers make her suspicious." Celie settled on the frayed seat.

He slid in beside her. "Seems she's passed that trait along to her granddaughter."

He was probably right, so she didn't bother arguing. It was later than she thought; she was surprised to see the streetlamps flickering outside. The day had nearly passed, and she hadn't accomplished anything. She glanced at her wrist before she remembered where her watch was.

Mark pulled it from his pocket. "Having withdrawal symptoms?" He handed it to her. "Don't worry—I'll take care of dinner. I have a great evening planned."

"Count me out. I've already wasted the better part of the day."

"Did you have a good time?"

She strapped the watch to her wrist while she considered, then nodded.

"So it wasn't wasted."

She frowned at his logic. "I thought the military lived and died by schedules."

"Not while we're on holiday leave. Don't you ever do things on the spur of the moment?"

She immediately thought of the Thanksgiving cruise. "I did, once."

His grin said he'd guessed what she'd remembered, and she was grateful he didn't ask her to elaborate.

"You've got to do better than that," he scolded, "or life will pass you by."

For a moment she considered letting his remark go unanswered, but it suddenly seemed important for him to understand her adherence to routines. "I spend my days helping women who've never planned for their future. They never imagined they'd be abandoned by their spouses, saddled with debts and a load of guilt they can't begin to handle."

"I'm not suggesting you go to the other extreme and plunge along blindly. There is a happy medium."

"I'm satisfied with my life just the way it is." At least she had been before she'd stepped aboard the cruise ship. Like a domino effect, that single reckless decision had made every moment of her routine back home seem bland and unsatisfying.

Mark pushed his packages to the floor and moved closer to her. "How do you know that if you haven't tried to live it any other way?" he said, running his finger over her windburned cheek.

The cab jolted as it struck a pothole, wedging the two of them closer together. Impossible, she thought, that in a car smelling of cigarette smoke and sweat, her body, insulated with inches of bulky clothing, would tighten with absolute physical awareness.

The cab's heater blasted air to the backseat. Feeling her cheeks flush, Celie cracked her window open an inch and willed herself to think of something other than the man beside her.

It was fruitless. With each measured breath she took to steady her pulse, she could smell his aftershave. Between her breaths, she could hear his own, slow and constant. Apparently his hormones weren't running haywire like hers.

"We should stop somewhere to buy some mulberry leaves."

She looked at him, trying to focus on what he said and not on his devilish smile, which only spelled trouble. "Pardon?"

"Mulberry leaves. You crush them and add them to a fire. Very aromatic."

Very tempting, but aromatherapy was the last thing she needed tonight. "No fire," she reminded him and herself. "No eggnog."

His smile deepened the laugh lines clustered around his eyes. "Spoilsport."

Chicken. Silently correcting him, she turned away and stared out the window. Sometimes, when she had nothing better to do, she fantasized about making love on a bed made with scarlet satin sheets in a room lit only by a flickering fire. Although the linen closet held nothing but sensible flannel and cotton bed linens, her bedroom had a fireplace. A little eggnog, a few crushed mulberry leaves—she could imagine how an evening beginning the way he described would end.

Then again, she didn't have to imagine. With breathtaking clarity, she remembered the first time he'd touched her, and the last.

Her thoughts were interrupted when the cab stopped in front of her house. She fumbled for her purse. "I've got it," Mark murmured, handing the cabby the fare.

The cold air shocked common sense back into her system as she walked to the house. Shannon's computer was loaded with sophisticated games, addictive ones that caused male guests to slip into a nightlong catatonic state once they started playing.

Tea, first, Celie decided as she walked into the foyer and stripped off her coat. Then she'd call out for a pizza. After dinner, she'd send Mark upstairs, challenging him to tackle one of the more difficult games, and she'd have the rest of the evening to herself.

While it might not be the evening she wanted, it certainly would be better in the long run.

Sitting in the kitchen, Mark watched Celie measure oolong leaves into a tea ball. She looked more relaxed than he'd seen her since he'd arrived.

Now would be the perfect time to confess he'd received the lettergram. Surely she'd understand why he'd played along with her assumption he hadn't received it, maybe even joke about it.

He'd explain how he boarded the cruise ship with the best intentions, determined to figure out his future but without a clue how until she burst into his life, a kindred soul appearing at dawn to witness the sunrise. He'd tell how she jolted him with her million-dollar smile—a figure of speech; he hadn't known it could be applied in the literal sense until he'd reached Boston and learned from Shannon that Celie was one of *the* Hargraves.

He heard something thunderous in her silence regarding her wealth, and knew they needed to discuss that, too. He'd sidestepped the issue long enough. To show he didn't gave a tinker's damn about money, he'd insist on a premarital contract.

First things first. He waited patiently while she steeped tea leaves in steaming water, not speaking until she'd carried the cup across the kitchen and sat in the chair opposite his.

"About the lettergram," he began.

She froze, the cup halfway to her mouth. "I knew you'd bring it up before you left."

She *knew?* His mind scrambled to look at things from a new perspective.

"I took a coward's way out, I admit, although now you understand why."

Spoken as if the reasons were obvious, he thought. "You're referring to the fact your family owns half of Boston?"

"My family has nothing to do with us." She lifted her hand when he started to talk. "I'm a realist, not a dreamer."

Like you. Even though she hadn't finished it, he clearly heard the rest of the sentence. "That didn't bother you the night I proposed," he reminded her.

Her cup rattled as she returned it to the saucer. "The idea of doing something so impulsive held a certain appeal. Of course the entire cruise Shannon was whispering in my ear to 'go for it.' She's a great one for bucking tradition."

By rights it was Shannon, feisty, beautiful, and leggy, who should have appealed to him. But destiny ruled otherwise. "And you're not?"

"I always knew what was expected of me, and why. Shannon couldn't wait to rebel. She eloped the day she turned eighteen."

It wasn't Shannon's past that interested him. "You must have done something to rock the proverbial boat."

"I didn't join Hargrave International after I passed the law boards. Grandmother was devastated; she'd had a gold company nameplate engraved as my graduation gift."

"We're more alike than you realize." He knew he was grasping at straws, but for the moment it was all he had. "I settled for Annapolis instead of buying into my dad's ranch. He never could understand why I'd prefer marching cadence to raising rattlesnakes."

He grinned at Celie's shudder. "My sentiments exactly. Unfortunately for Dad, the great rattlesnake-stew craze never materialized, so that venture failed. Same with the exotic cactus farming and desert dude-ranching. He's breeding chinchilla now, although the animal lovers of the world are bringing that to an unprofitable end. Doesn't matter; his heart's never really been in settling down. One of these days, he'll do something he's been dreaming about for years—travel to the Yukon and pan for gold."

She stirred her untasted tea. "You told me you came from an average American family."

If memory served him right, so had she. "I didn't want to scare you away, although at the time I didn't know two of your ancestors signed the Declaration of Independence."

She frowned as if she couldn't understand the connection.

He tried to explain. "I come from a long line of dabblers. As far as I know, none of my forefathers made a dent in the business world. Then again, I don't even know my grandma's maiden name. She claims her parents were Gypsies, that they left her on an orphanage doorstep the day she was born. Characters like that blight my family tree."

Since he'd half expected her to cringe with disgust, her laugh shocked him. "I think it would be easier making a family name than trying to live up to one," she told him. "No one's been reminding you daily that your grandfather revolutionized the auto industry by offering his workers paid vacations, that your great-grandfather patented a refining process that steel mills still use, that his father's cotton warehousing stabilized the New England economy following the Civil War. The point being not what *they* did, but what *you* can do to top them."

"Tough being rich," Mark teased. "What have you done to top them?"

"Not a thing. The day I decided to bypass corporate law, Grandmother gave up hope. For a while she concentrated her efforts on my cousins, although at the moment I'm back in the spotlight. She says it's time I find a husband to 'beget' a son."

He thought that had gone the way of prearranged marriages. "You're not serious."

"The order has been given to the Hargrave clan to find me a suitable husband."

"What's considered suitable?"

"In Grandmother's eyes? Blue-blooded and monied."

Two strikes against him, he figured, watching Celie carry her cup to the sink. "And in yours?"

"Mutual goals and interests."

"And you've gone thirty years without meeting your perfect

match." He couldn't help feeling smug. The conversation couldn't be flowing smoother had he engineered it himself.

She rinsed the cup before she answered. "I've met four. You had me name them this afternoon."

"But you didn't find your soul mate, did you? Out of a million men, there's only one in the world for you."

"Stop preaching predestination."

Walking to the sink, he watched her wipe her hands on a towel. "There were at least four hundred single men aboard that cruise ship," he said, determined to make his point. "How many did you share the sunrises with?"

"There were only seven sunrises to see."

Watching the memory warm her smile, Mark clasped his hands behind his back to keep from touching her. "You shared them all with me."

"Only because everyone else was too busy partying to even notice a sun rises over the Caribbean Sea."

"Only because no one else cared." Mark took the towel she'd been wringing and tossed it onto the counter. "You did, I did. Soul mates."

"Convoluted logic," she protested, her smile diluting her criticism.

Forgetting his resolve not to touch her, he caught her hand in his. "Still not convinced, are you? Let's try again. You've thought about marriage at least four times, right?" At the moment he found it impossible to include himself in the tally. "Why did you back out each and every time?"

"Because I didn't feel compelled to make a commitment to share the rest of my life with someone. I certainly don't need the financial security."

Good, he thought, because that was the one thing he couldn't offer. "There are other reasons for marrying."

"I suppose."

He grinned at her skepticism. "Your grandma's stated an obvious one—an heir to the Hargrave name."

"This being the nineteen-nineties, being a single mother is no longer socially unacceptable."

Maybe not to society, but he could tell Celie personally didn't think much of the idea. He laced his fingers with hers. "Then there's a feeling you couldn't possibly live without that other person, in or out of bed."

"I wouldn't know about that." Refusing to meet his gaze, she tried to tug her hand free but only pulled him closer.

"It's a feeling that keeps you awake at night, makes you stumble through your days." He caught her chin and turned her face toward his so she had no choice but to look at him. "Sometimes it causes you to panic and do irrational things."

"Calling things quits is hardly irrational." She knew her voice lacked its usual overwhelming confidence, so she drew a deep breath, then rushed a question. "Do you like computer games?"

Watching her eyes darken, he tried to focus on what she said. "Hmmm?"

"Computer games."

"I despise them," he whispered, pressing his lips to her flushed cheek.

"Pizza?" She tried one last desperate distraction before his mouth found hers.

Just a kiss, she told herself, yet she found it evolving into something intangible, something soothing and promise-filled and satisfying, even while it made her ache for more. Her body pliant, she moved against him.

Underneath her sweater, his hands felt like hot silk flowing up and down her back, urging her closer still. Trembling when he touched her breast, she felt the need to touch and taste him unbearable as sensations swamped her.

Caught in the magic of his kiss, she fumbled with his top shirt button, nearly crying out when he gripped her arms and set her away.

"Perfect match, don't you think?" he asked, his voice hoarse.

She'd almost lost control. Again. The realization made her resist the emotional whirlwind inside her, and she marshaled the warnings hovering in the corners of her mind. She tried to glare and catch her breath at the same time, but failed at both. "Just because you kiss well doesn't mean we're destined for a life together."

She expected him to remind her that he'd been the first to break the kiss. Instead, he smiled and shook his head. "Back to the mutual goals and interests, are we?"

Where he found the strength to tease, she couldn't imagine. Her own legs were so shaky she didn't dare move away from the counter. "We don't have many, do we?"

"Right now I'd be content to watch desert sunrises the rest of my life, my woman at my side, my children on my knee. How about you?"

Such a simplistic view of life, utterly irrational in its appeal. She knew she should get well out of touching distance, go upstairs, sit at her desk, and immerse herself in her work.

As if he sensed her change in mood, he shook his head. "No way, darlin'. I'm taking you to dinner."

Darlin'? No man had called her that before, no man had used that voice, rich and low and filled with promises of things to come. If she wasn't careful, she'd melt into his arms, damn the consequences. "We'll call out for pizza," she countered. "I have work to do."

Yet the way her pulse pounded and her hands shook, she wouldn't be able to give work her full concentration. *Any* concentration at all, for that matter. What she needed was a diversion, something loud and noisy to overtax her senses. "Somewhere close," she conceded, since he hadn't yet agreed to the pizza.

Mark nodded. "We'll be back in an hour. Charlie recommended a place nearby."

Warming her car's engine, Celie watched through the windshield as Mark brushed away the snow. He wouldn't tell her where they were going; in fact, he wouldn't tell her anything except to dress casually. That eliminated Charlie's favorite haunt, the exclusive Bay Tower Room and, she hoped, any intimately atmosphered restaurants in the area.

Prudence, that's what she needed, to keep Mark at arm's length, to focus on small talk. People never needed to be persuaded to talk about themselves. She'd get Mark to relate the highlights of his service career, and the evening would be over before she knew it.

He climbed into the passenger seat and switched on the overhead light. Spotting the flakes of snow glistening on his shoulders, she reached to brush them away, then caught herself and instead tuned in to a classical radio station. She put her car in gear. "Where are we going?"

Fishing out a paper from his coat pocket, he read the address aloud.

She nodded. "That's near Boston College." A student hangout, no doubt, complete with garish lighting, rock music, beer, and mediocre overgreased food. She couldn't have suggested a less-romantic place herself.

Spouting trivia, she pointed out landmarks as she drove, not providing him an opportunity to talk until she finally pulled into a plowed parking lot and stopped the car. "Now what?"

Mark dug two tickets from his wallet.

"Hockey game?" Celie asked, thinking that would be even better than a restaurant. It would be rather difficult to talk about anything with a crowd roaring around them.

Mark swung open his car door. "Holiday bonfire on the Quad. We're going to roast hot dogs and marshmallows."

"Outside? It's fourteen degrees and falling."

"I'll keep you warm," he promised, climbing out of the car.

That sent her scrambling from her seat before he reached the driver's side. "I'm Boston born and bred," she reminded him, slamming her door and wrapping a scarf around her neck. "I can weather anything."

Seven

At a makeshift booth set up on the snow-covered commons, Mark traded his tickets for two sticks. Handing one to Celie, he watched her inspect the whittled end. "You've roasted hot dogs before, haven't you?"

He grinned when she didn't answer, deciding not to reveal that when he was a boy, hot dogs had been the Friday dinner staple at his home. "Have you ever eaten one?"

"Of course."

One might be the definitive answer, he realized. He certainly wasn't going to need an American Express Gold Card to make an impression tonight.

After stripping off his gloves, he stuffed them into his pocket before picking up two foot-long wieners encased in buns. He handed one to Celie. "You'll manage better without your mittens. Just do what I do, and no one will be the wiser."

He slid the meat from the bun onto the pointed end of the stick, watching to make sure she did the same. Then he elbowed his way through the crowd milling about the fire, found a good spot, and motioned Celie to stand in front of him. "You like yours rare, medium, or well done?"

"Whatever you're having."

He preferred his scorched. At the condiment table, he piled his bun with every topping offered, trying not to grin when Celie squirted only a thin line of catsup onto hers. "Drinks," he said when she finished. He guided her to a nearby table.

She chose a cup of mulled cider. It felt good against her cold fingers but was too hot to sip. "Where are the tables?"

"We eat picnic-style."

When he smiled at her, her breath hitched. She'd been naive to think atmosphere set the tone for romance. Candlelit tables and mellow wine in lead-crystal goblets couldn't possibly make her more vulnerable to that smile.

Slowly she became aware of the surroundings again—people jostling past, the bonfire crackling in the night. Yet she couldn't stop watching him while she finished her sandwich.

He wasn't the type of man she'd consider, if the day ever came when she did decide to marry. She'd choose someone who'd fit in with her lifestyle, someone who left for work early and came home late, a man who'd understand when she brought work home because his own briefcase would be packed with papers. Just as important, he would be someone who'd tolerate her grandmother's penchant for interfering. Celie doubted Mark had the patience to handle the criticism and advice the older woman doled out to family and acquaintances.

He pulled her toward a table. "How many marshmallows do you want?"

When she couldn't answer, he arched his eyebrows. "Just what does your family eat at picnics?

"Steamed crab, corn on the cob."

"That silver spoon in your mouth is getting tarnished tonight, isn't it?" He tossed her a plastic sandwich bag of marshmallows, pocketing one himself before they headed back to the fire. He browned a few, then handed her the stick and watched her taste one. "How is it?"

She washed the mouthful down with cider. "Tasteless."

"Spoken from one with good taste. They'll never replace chocolate torte, but they do get you into the spirit of things." When he finished toasting the rest, he looked around. "Let's go over there."

He ushered her toward a cluster of birch trees at the fringe of the bonfire light, clearing a stone bench of its layer of snow before he offered her a seat.

"Shouldn't you be pressing palms for Charlie?" she asked as she sat. "He must want something in exchange for the tickets—he never gives things without strings attached."

"They were a gift." Mark settled beside her. "This is Christmas, remember? We're just supposed to be having a good time. Warm enough?"

Whether she was or not, she couldn't say. She couldn't think of anything that mattered when he looked at her that way.

He glanced around him, his expression apologetic. "You're probably used to soft lights and music on your dinner dates.

Not wanting to admit he was right, she laughed. "This certainly is unique."

He laced his fingers through hers. "I want to make this your best Christmas ever."

"You've already given me a Thanksgiving I'll never forget." When he pressed her fingers to his lips, she couldn't stop herself from tracing his mouth, couldn't keep the memories from tumbling through her mind. "Who could ask for anything more?"

"You could."

She withdrew her hand. Her rational mind warned her to steer the conversation back to saner, safer topics, but as long as he sat a breath away and watched her with eyes that seemed to see into her mind, she couldn't listen to reason. "I have everything I need."

"Except me."

Smiling at his persistence, she shook her head.

"Why don't you give me a chance?"

As if it were that easy. "A chance? You're not talking about the Irish sweepstakes, you're talking about my life."

"Our lives," he corrected. "Although I have the feeling I'd have a better chance playing the sweepstakes. You must have some outstanding expectations for your husband-to-be."

"Not outstanding, just reasonable."

"Such as?"

"Sense of humor. Intelligent. Supportive. Loyal. Understanding." She stopped because he was all of those, and she supposed he'd tell her so just to prove his point. "Stop looking so skeptical," she said before he could say anything. "You must have some characteristics you want to find in a wife."

"Look in a mirror and you'll see them all."

A line, she told herself, probably one he had tossed to every fiancée he had. No doubt they'd all reacted the way she had, skeptical yet unable to bite back a pleased smile. "I'm serious.

"So am I. They say your ideal partner is the one who crumbles all your expectations. It's true. You're not at all the woman I imagined myself marrying, but you are the woman I'm going to marry."

Ignoring his last statement, she concentrated on the former. "That doesn't make sense."

"We're not talking sense, we're talking love."

"You're talking utter nonsense."

He took her hand, turning it palm up. "Maybe you'd listen to a third party. My grandma reads palms."

Her breasts tightened when he traced the life line running from the base of her thumb to her little finger. "A third party should be unbiased," she reminded him.

"She has my best interests at heart, but that wouldn't keep her from speaking up if I've made a mistake."

Stunned by her physical response to the simple whisper of his fingers across her palm, she had to swallow twice before she spoke. "A fortune-teller says only what you want to hear."

"In this case, she has."

Her concentration slipping, she found it difficult to focus on his words. "Has what?"

"Sent me a letter saying you're the one."

"That's crazy." Celie curled her fingers to stop his from exploring and struggled to cling to her argument. "She doesn't even know me."

"My point exactly."

She closed her eyes as he nuzzled her knuckles, wishing she could summon enough energy to resist the desire shimmering through her like fluid heat. Whispering her name, he slid his hand to her neck and drew her face closer to his. With a sigh, she surrendered, tunneling her fingers through his hair, losing herself in the sensual power of his kiss.

When he cradled her in his arms and made a world just for two, she responded like an addict deprived too long of a fix. But unhurried and giving as it was, the kiss didn't begin to satisfy her need; it only taunted her, leaving a bold craving for more.

He lifted his head, his breath mingling with hers. "Ready for the sing-along?"

Feeling like a pile of putty, she inched away and pulled off her hat to finger-comb her hair. How he could recover so quickly, she couldn't imagine, although she supposed with his five previous fiancées, practice probably made perfect. She tried to harness the jealousy flaring through her, but didn't succeed. "I don't sing. Not even in the shower."

"Everyone sings Christmas carols." He slid his arm around her shoulders, keeping her close to him. "This is great, isn't it? Just like a Currier and Ives print. Do you paint?"

"You're confusing me with Shannon. She paints, sings, plays a mean jazz piano." It pleased her to hear that her voice was steady, even if her pulse wasn't.

He quirked a brow. "You must have some redeeming assets."

"None I can think of offhand." The activities around her lacked something, and she suddenly realized what it was. There should be children roasting hot dogs, creating snow angels, crowding with their parents into a bell-strung sleigh for a wintery moonlit ride.

"One asset." Resting his hand on her knee, Mark drummed his fingers. "Some charming trait our children will inherit."

Coincidence, she told herself, digging her mittens from her pocket and pulling them on. He couldn't possibly have seen the picture her mind had created. "We aren't going to have children."

"I guess not, at this rate," he said gloomily. "Who'll sit in the backseat of the station wagon?"

"You told me you owned a Datsun."

"We'll have to trade it for a wood-paneled wagon, or a mini-van. You have to, after you're married. It's tradition, just like a wedding ring, a honeymoon. We haven't talked about those things, either."

Aboard ship she'd pieced together an entire wedding, honeymoon and all, wistful thinking she'd abandoned by the time reality dragged her home to Boston. Now she kept her voice light and teasing, matching his. "Talk's cheap."

"Diamonds aren't. It's a good thing I haven't squandered my pay all these years on hedonistic pleasures. I imagine your grandma will insist on the Hope Diamond."

"At least."

"I'll manage," Mark said cheerfully. "Now the honeymoon— that's a different story. What in the world haven't you seen?"

"Let's see . . . rule out Paris, Cairo, Honolulu . . ." She ticked off several more places on her fingers before she shook her head. "I've been everywhere, I guess."

Mark sighed. "Where would you like to go?"

For several minutes she considered. "Disney World," she finally decided, choking back a laugh at his startled expression. "That's exactly how my grandmother looked when I told her I wanted to go there instead of Paris on my sixteenth birthday. No need to say we went to France instead. I promised myself when I grew up I'd go to Disney World."

"You and a million other people," Mark muttered. "I had something more secluded in mind, maybe a deserted island tucked away in the Caribbean, where we could build a lean-to and live on coconuts."

That so closely resembled her dream honeymoon she stared open-mouthed for a few seconds before she collected her wits. Another coincidence. Maybe her grandmother was right—people found coincidences wherever they looked. "Forget it. I'm a city girl and I intend to have my honeymoon blessed with running water and electricity."

He looked skeptical. "Here I pegged you for a nature lover."

"Only from afar." A snowball plopped on the bench beside her. She ducked when another whizzed by her ear. "We're in the middle of a battle zone," she said, noticing the members of a sorority and fraternity who had squared off on either side of the bench.

"Truce," Mark called, grabbing Celie's hand as he stood.

They found a spot on the ground near the fire. Shrugging off his coat, he spread it over the snow before they sat. She glanced around her as she settled and was surprised to recognize several businessmen. Alumni present out of loyalty, she supposed. She knew all about loyalty; she'd attended hundreds of functions solely to represent the Hargrave name. None had been this pleasant.

"I'm glad Charlie handed over his tickets," Mark said. "He said he wanted me to see Boston's best."

"Boston's best?" She thought of a dozen places she could show Mark. "He should have sent you to Salem; there's a mariners' exhibit at the Peabody Museum."

"Great." Mark blew on his hands and rubbed them together. "We'll go tomorrow."

Leaning back on her elbows, Celie watched the flickering fire sweep shadows over his face, making him look darker, almost mysterious. For an instant, she thought maybe she could see a trace of Gypsy blood. Not, she reminded herself objectively, that being dark and handsome had anything to do with matters. After all, she'd dated some of the city's best-looking men and they'd left her . . . well, not cold, but not like this, not overwhelmed with a feeling that threatened to dissolve everything she'd held to be important until three weeks ago. The awareness tempted her to set new priorities, to reach willingly and wantonly for the unknown.

Only it wasn't the unknown that attracted her. It was Mark.

He was still waiting for her to respond to his question about the museum. "Tomorrow's Monday," she reminded him. "I go back to work."

"You can't take a day off?"

Refusing to even consider the thought, she shook her head. "I've already wasted today. I don't want to cultivate a bad habit."

"Let me talk to your boss. I'll tell him I have only a few more days of shore leave and I intend to make every moment count."

"My supervisor is a woman, and you'll do no such thing." This close to the fire, she felt warm, despite the arctic temperature around her. She unzipped her jacket and loosened the scarf around her neck.

"You'll invite her to the wedding, won't you?"

"I keep my personal and professional life separate. Besides, there isn't going to be a wedding to invite her to."

"That's right; you wanted to elope."

Celie wrapped her arms around her knees, his reference to a conversation they'd shared aboard the ship sending a burst of color into her cheeks. When he proposed, she'd actually suggested they enlist the captain to perform the ceremony onboard. Mark had been the one to suggest they wait until spring, when his navy tour would end and their families could attend.

"We could fly west tonight," he coaxed. "I hear there's a chapel in Las Vegas that conducts drive-through ceremonies. We'll have videotapes made, one for your mother, one for mine."

She could imagine her family gathered around the television, shocked into silence as they watched.

"We'll take your Aunt Louise along as a witness," Mark added. "I think she's secretly longing to kick up her heels."

Louise would love it, Celie knew. No longer able to resist, she laughed aloud. "What about my grandmother?"

"We'll bring her back a souvenir. Salt-and-pepper shakers in the shape of miniature slot machines, something she can display in the Hargrave trophy case."

"And my mother?"

"No problem. She'll be gaining a son."

Celie sighed and rested her chin on her knees. "You've thought of everything, haven't you?"

"All I need is the bride." He touched her face, with gentle pressure turning it toward his. "Your cheeks are getting chapped."

Strange his cold fingers could leave such a trail of heat as they drifted over her skin. Odd how just a touch could make her heart leap and pour life into her body. When his thumb traced the line of her jaw, she tipped her head back, allowing his fingers access to explore the pulse throbbing in her throat.

This being college territory, no doubt the cider had been laced with liquor, she decided, which would explain her lassitude, her reluctance to pull away. Alcohol obscures good judgment. Hadn't she preached that a hundred times to clients she counseled at the shelter?

But honesty nudged her, forcing her to admit alcohol wasn't the only thing that threatened good judgment, nor was it at fault here. She was too old to hide behind flimsy excuses. The only thing scattering her common sense to the north wind was Mark Edwards.

If she leaned just an inch closer, she could put her head on his shoulder, forget the noisy crowd milling around, blot out the smell of beer and smoke, and kiss him.

She wanted nothing more.

Yet she heard herself babbling as some protective device kicked in to keep her mind occupied with other less-satisfying but safer, saner thoughts. "Have you thought about piloting a cruise ship after you retire? I remember your saying it seemed like a job you'd enjoy."

He straightened the collar of her jacket. "That's a job for a single man, someone who wouldn't worry about leaving a wife alone for months at a time."

"You don't have a wife."

"I will soon."

He spoke with such finality, she bit her lip, trying to tamp down a gush of guilt as something occurred to her. "You haven't put your future on hold thinking I'm going to marry you?"

"You *are* going to marry me."

She wriggled her toes in her boots and flexed her fingers inside her mittens, but the distractions failed to keep her from smiling. "Are you always this single-minded?"

"No, but then the right woman has never walked into my life before. Or out of it, for that matter."

The student band that had assembled in the middle of the Quad struck up a chorus of "Jingle Bells," forestalling her from arguing the point. She hugged her knees and listened to Mark's baritone as he joined the sing-along.

His same qualities which appealed to her during the Thanksgiving cruise threatened to seduce her now—his sense of humor, his ability to laugh at himself, his willingness to compromise, his stubbornness that she felt could match her own.

She tried to remember if she'd felt this way with the others she'd considered marrying, but found comparison impossible. They'd faded to colorless memories in her mind, shoved into cobwebbed corners along with recollections of debutante ball escorts and prom dates.

Illogical as it sounded, she felt her past had been severed, no longer intertwined with her future. On the cruise, she felt a lifetime away from Boston, and she'd pretended to be reckless and carefree, acting as if she didn't have a legacy of Hargrave tradition to uphold.

Mark didn't have to pretend. He looked as comfortable here as he had the previous night circling the ballroom floor, as he had aboard ship bending over the sink to be closer to the mirror, wearing little more than shaving cream. Like a love-struck teenager, she'd envied the razor as it whispered along his jaw, and as soon as he'd rinsed his face she'd followed the same path with her fingers and then kisses . . .

She couldn't refrain from sighing even as she vowed to forget the memory. From the corner of her eye, she saw Mark watching her intently, as if he could read her soul.

Then again, maybe he simply knew her too well. He'd countered every argument with logic too simple for her to reason against. Maybe, in the scheme of things, the affair aboard the ship had been a prelude, not an interlude.

Maybe he was right—perhaps fate did grab you by the heart and jerk you to where you belonged. Right now, looking at him beside her, she couldn't think of a more appropriate place to be. Maybe caution and common sense had nothing to do with it, maybe marriage had nothing to do with love and everything to do with finding a mate. Not someone perfect, but someone compatible, someone to laugh and cry with, someone who'd warm the bed on cold nights and warm your heart when life didn't.

All things considered, she certainly could find worse than Mark. She doubted whether she could find better.

And she'd be the first to admit—outside Grandmother's hearing, of course—that her biological clock was ticking louder than ever before. Obviously, Mark came from a loving family and would know better than she how to rear a happy child. He'd be a good father, a dependable husband.

The magic, the passion she'd experienced aboard ship would fade, and then their life would settle into a comfortable predictable pattern. Not a marriage of convenience, but one of suitability, and they were well suited to each other. He hadn't demanded she give up anything, hadn't expected her to compromise her principles in any way. In return, she'd do the same.

She stared at him, biting her lower lip while she considered. After all the false starts she'd experienced, she wondered if she'd ever trust her judgment to find the right man to marry. Now she felt relief that the decision had been so simple, almost yanked from her hands by an unknown force.

Without breaking eye contact, Mark caught her around the shoulders and inched her closer. She couldn't imagine how irresistible she looked, he thought. The chill in the air had swept color into her cheeks, made her eyes sparkle like gold-flecked emeralds. Shadows from the fire painted interesting hollows on her cheeks, ones he wanted to map with his mouth. It might be a small victory she'd slid closer, willingly, without even a token protest. Then again, he reminded himself stoically, she might simply be chilled.

And the sigh . . . he was torn between kissing her and asking what weighed on her mind. While he contemplated, she looked at him, her tilted chin practically challenging him to do something.

Unable to resist the dare, he leaned closer. Her lips were cold, but the kiss packed a punch to his senses, making him despise the strangers around him who deprived him of the privacy he suddenly hungered for.

Her lips parted and softened under his. Clinging to his control, he pulled away. There was a time and place for what he wanted. This was neither.

"Let's go," he said, his voice so low that for a moment he doubted whether she'd heard him.

She had, and allowed him to help her to her feet. He found himself brushing his lips over hers again when he bent his head to fasten her coat's zipper. His breath hitched at the tenderness he saw reflected in her eyes.

Nearly cursing when she handed him the car keys, he climbed behind the wheel. Even though the streets had been plowed, they remained slick. A novice to northern winters, driving in snow would require his utmost concentration, when all he wanted to think about was the potency he'd sampled that served as a heady promise of more to come.

After warming the engine, he switched off the heater because her perfume filled the car, teasing him to guess all the places she applied it. Pulse points at her neck, elbows, behind her knees . . .

just the thought sent his heart thudding. Trying to concentrate on driving, he kept his gaze trained on the road, determined not to listen to her breathing too fast and shallow. Ragged, like his own.

He'd reached a milestone today by bridging a gap in her resistance. A precarious link, true, and not all that he'd hoped to achieve, but only a fool would fail to seize the advantage.

Considering her future, Celie rode home in silence. There were problems to iron out, concessions to be made, goals to be set. She'd insist on a long courtship, not only to see whether they really meshed, but to discover any insurmountable problems before they'd made a commitment.

She hadn't taken a day off work the entire year; certainly the staff could function without her tomorrow while she tended to personal matters. She and Mark would sit down and logically plot their future, talk about houses and children and wedding guest lists.

Still preoccupied with plans when she walked inside her house, she pulled off her coat and hat. There was so much to do. Maybe they should start tackling things tonight. She'd ease into her announcement over an evening snack, she decided, turning around to face him. "Coffee?"

"No." His refusal was soft, his voice husky. His gaze wandered over her face and her static-filled hair before settling on her mouth.

"I'm sure Shannon wouldn't mind if you opened her Courvoisier." Even as she spoke, she realized it wasn't liquor he wanted, but something more intoxicating, more satisfying, twice as addictive. The desire darkening his eyes turned her blood to liquid fire, and she knew if he crossed the room, she wouldn't be able to turn away.

He stood where he was, his hands behind his back, his back against the foyer door. "Come here, Celie."

Forcing her to make a conscious choice, she realized. Anticipation stole her breath as she glided across the room and stopped before him. She trembled when at first he didn't touch her but only looked, then trembled more when he framed her face in his hands.

Although her pulse thundered in her ears, she heard him whisper her name, his voice a caress that swept over her. Resting her palms on his chest, she let her fingers absorb the rapid beat of his heart, then closed her eyes as he kissed the bridge of her nose, her eyebrow, her temple.

The glide of his mouth on hers made her shiver with delight. His tongue flirted with hers, flaring consuming need deep inside her to life. She moved closer, her frustration at the layers of clothing separating them barely tempered by a heady sense of expectation.

Gasping with pleasure when his hands slid under her sweater to cradle her breasts, she trailed her fingers over his back, exploring inch by inch the muscle and bone beneath his shirt. Desire shimmered through her when he unclasped her bra.

"Mark, wait . . ." Through a mist of raw emotion, she heard the plea tumble from her throat. First she needed to tell him of her decision. She owed it to him, although she waited one more moment, tilting her head while he nuzzled her neck.

"What?" he whispered against her skin.

"I've decided I'll marry you."

The last thing she expected him to do was still his hands and stare into her eyes.

"I've thought about it. You were right—we will be good together." Although his shuttered expression made it impossible for her to judge his reaction, instinct suddenly warned her to proceed with caution.

For several moments he said nothing. He smoothed her sweater back in place while watching her, then let his hands rest on her shoulders. "Sounds pragmatic."

"We need to sit down tomorrow and discuss things."

"Things?" he repeated, drawing his brows together.

"Complications we might encounter. Problems—"

"Good night, Celie." He nudged her toward the stairway.

She stood her ground, seeking to read a message in his eyes, needing something to explain the frustration, anything to ease the knot of disappointment tightening her throat that made speech nearly impossible. She found nothing.

"Go to bed," he said.

She swallowed to control her panic. Maybe this had been his goal the past few days, to make her feel what he must have felt when she turned him down. Self-preservation demanded she cross the room and march up the stairs without giving him a second thought. She was horrified to find herself on the brink of tears, and she blinked them away. "I thought you'd be happy."

He jammed his hands into his pockets. "I'd be happy if there were three little words tacked onto your agreement."

It took her a moment to realize what he meant. "I'm not going to lie and say I based my decision on love," she told him. "I do think we're suited for each other."

"Suited." He muttered the word, shaking his head. "You make it sound like we're forming a business."

She tipped her chin defensively. "Marriage is a partnership."

"I told you I'm old-fashioned, as in first comes love, *then* comes marriage."

Since she hadn't expected him to refuse her offer, she didn't have a defense prepared. "Perhaps love, whatever it is, will follow."

"Not as long as you keep that emotional barrier in place."

"This is a practical decision." She was relieved her voice sounded calm, not reflecting the humiliation she felt that he'd turned down her offer. "My emotions have nothing to do with it."

"Your emotions have everything to do with it. This is a marriage, not a corporate merger.

She stood there, hopelessly lost, wanting him to take her in his arms again. She wasn't sure how to ask. "I don't know what you want," she whispered miserably.

"All . . . or nothing. Good night, Celie."

Unable to think of anything else to say, she turned and went upstairs.

Ten minutes later, she replayed the scene over in her mind as she brushed her teeth, trying to forget what an outright fool she'd been. Had she waited until tomorrow to tell him of her decision, she'd be in his arms now instead of facing another cold night alone.

Rinsing her mouth, she stared at her reflection in the mirror. With every inch of skin below her neck except her fingers and toes swathed in white flannel, she couldn't look less alluring. She'd chosen the nightgown without thinking, although she supposed her subconscious was mocking her celibacy.

Mock away, she thought. Her cheeks burned from a combination of wind and whisker burn, but her pride suffered even more.

She tried not to think about what had happened, or what hadn't happened, as she headed down the hall toward her bedroom.

"I switched on your electric blanket. Figured your bed might feel colder than usual tonight."

His husky voice startled her. She could distinguish his outline in Shannon's bed but realized he had the advantage because she stood illuminated in the pool of hallway light.

"Thank you." She kept her reply dignified, not wanting to reveal her discomfort that he'd invaded her bedroom, if only for a moment. She resisted an impulse to flee into her bedroom and dodge any discussion about what occurred downstairs. If he wanted revenge, she'd let him get his fill. Then they'd be even; she'd jilted him, he'd rejected her.

"You look pretty in that gown. Old-fashioned."

"Thank you." Her vocabulary had become terribly limited. She searched for something to say, something flip and original, to show what happened downstairs meant absolutely nothing to her. Startled, she blinked when he switched on the bedside lamp.

He sat in the bed, bare-chested, the covers tumbling carelessly to his waist. "Maybe we can pick up where we left off a few minutes ago," he said, his teasing smile telling her it wasn't really talking he wanted to do.

"No." Her tongue seemed dry, sticking inconveniently to the roof of her mouth as physical awareness swept over her, weakening her resolve to leave well enough alone, at least for tonight.

His grin disappeared, replaced by an expression so intense she wanted to cross the room and slip back into his arms. "I love you, Celie," he said softly.

Had she been less honorable, she could mimic his words, if only to assuage the fire he'd again kindled under her skin. But they weren't words she could toss lightly, if at all.

"Good night, Mark." Before he could persuade her to stay, before she could persuade herself to stay, she fled down the hallway, nearly tripping on the gown billowing around her ankles.

Eight

Mark didn't settle back against the pillows until he heard Celie's door latch. He hadn't slept well the first night he'd arrived, hearing her move about her room, foolishly hoping with every creak of her bed she would change her mind and come tell him so.

Tonight, sleep would be a lost cause altogether. Unhindered by ethics, he could have taken her downstairs. The thought forced him to clench his fists and practice stress-reducing breathing exercises while he reminded himself he wanted her to stay in his bed for a lifetime, not a night.

He wanted a marriage based on love, not logic. And even though he hadn't questioned her decision or asked her to rationalize it, she'd presented it the way he imagined she'd handle a business proposition. Sensible, void of passion.

Somehow she figured he'd fit into her life, and he didn't intend to be a fixture. When they married they'd start from square one and build a life together based on a till-death-do-us-part commitment.

He wanted to crawl into her heart so deep she'd die before she would leave him, and he wanted her to want him the same way he wanted her, so much so that she'd put his needs ahead of hers, if necessary. The way he'd just done downstairs.

Still, all the justifying in the world didn't alter his physical state. There was no way he could fall asleep tonight with the feel of her skin still on his hands, the taste of her mouth still on his lips. Kicking away the sheets, he climbed out of bed and headed down the hall.

In the bathroom he stripped, twisting on the cold-water faucet before he stepped under the pounding spray of the shower. He clenched his teeth as water sluiced over his back. Either it ran colder here in Boston, or he was getting older, less tolerant of life's minor discomforts.

Older. She looked like a teenager tonight with the nightgown floating around her. He'd turn forty in the summer; she hadn't yet celebrated her thirtieth birthday.

A decade apart. Ten years ago he hadn't given a second thought—or even a first one, for that matter—to settling down. Times had changed. His needs had changed, forever altered the day he'd seen her silhouetted against the radiant sunrise. All his grandma's preachings about predestiny sprang to life in that instant.

In his forty years, he'd never wanted a woman so much.

Not a woman, but *one* woman. Celie by his side, in his bed, mothering his children, growing old with him.

Closing his eyes, he turned and lifted his face to the water while he plotted the next fifty years of his life, until her pounding on the door brought him back to reality. Wrenching the faucet closed, he swiped water from his eyes. "What?"

"You've been in there nearly half an hour. You're going to run out of hot water.

Figuring it imprudent to reveal he'd been using only cold, he stepped from the tub and grabbed a folded towel from the pile she'd left on the sink. The shower had done little to improve his physical or mental state. He found scarce consolation in the fact she couldn't sleep, either. "I wouldn't mind that coffee now, if the offer still stands," he called through the door.

Five minutes later, his hair still damp, he walked into the kitchen. She'd hidden the modest nightgown under a quilted robe and had tied her hair into a single braid. A plate of cookies and his coffee sat ready on the kitchen table.

He frowned, both at the single mug and the wary way she watched him. "Feel free to join me," he said. "I promise to keep my lust under control."

She didn't smile as she slipped into a chair. "I'll make arrangements to take off work tomorrow. We could drive to Salem, to the museum, if you want."

A peace offering, he supposed, and he nodded to show there were no hard feelings. If she wasn't going to bring up what happened a few hours ago, neither was he. Stirring sugar into his coffee, he studied her as she drew random patterns on the tablecloth.

"Will this museum trip be like an official date?" he asked.

She flushed but didn't look away from his gaze. "I thought we could get to know each other better."

"I'm honored," he said solemnly. "Especially since Charlie told me you were wedded to your job and never miss a day's work unless you're sick as a dog."

He meant it as a compliment but saw her bristle with anger. "Charlie's never volunteered for anything in his life," she said tartly. "He can't imagine why I feel obligated, to put in regular hours if I'm not being paid a salary."

"Why do you?"

"Because when they're deserted, women need child support, food stamps, subsidized rent, whatever else is available to get them on their feet again. Sometimes they come in with only the clothes on their back. In many ways they'd be better off as widows than as deserted spouses. Maybe my mother didn't have a job, but at least she had my father's military insurance to pay off the bills."

He latched onto the first bit of information she'd volunteered about her family. "Your dad was military?"

"Infantry, Vietnam." Celie chose a cookie from the plate.

He proceeded carefully since he suspected she'd grasp at the first opportunity to turn the focus of the conversation back his way. "Your mother must have married quite young."

"The day she turned eighteen."

"I'm surprised your grandma let her go at that tender age."

Mother ran away when she was seventeen. Or rather, ran off. She wanted to be a flower child, so she joined a commune in upper-state New York and changed her name to Summer Zephyr."

Mark grinned, finding it impossible to imagine elegant Katherine draped in glass beads and a caftan. "Your grandma must have turned gray overnight."

"No, that happened after Aunt Louise smuggled my mother's birth certificate from the library safe for the wedding."

He found himself liking Louise more and more. "So your parents were flower children. What was your father like?"

"Grandmother's worst dreams come true. He couldn't hold a job and finally decided to join the Army. Not the best decision in the mid-sixties, but he and mother thought Grandmother had the contacts to keep him out of Vietnam. She did, but she wouldn't."

She sat reciting the story as if it had happened to someone else. Somehow she'd convinced herself she'd moved beyond the loss, and Mark knew she wouldn't appreciate him pointing out otherwise. "Your father was killed in action?" he prompted.

"Twenty-four years ago. The telegram came on Christmas Eve. The next day Mother packed everything we owned into an old steamer trunk. I remember crying because I just knew Santa wouldn't be able to find me again if we moved.

"That was the least of my mother's worries; she hadn't finished high school and had to support us both. My father's insurance settled the bills, but that was about it, so she crawled back home and begged for Grandmother's forgiveness."

"She took her back?"

"Under certain conditions. She hired a tutor so Mother could earn her high school diploma, and she insisted I be turned over for proper finishing. They didn't believe in such things at the commune, so I didn't know how to act like a young lady."

If he touched her he knew he wouldn't be able to stop until he'd driven the bad memories away in the best way he knew how. So he picked up his mug instead and took a sip of coffee. "They shipped you off to boarding school?"

She grimaced. "No, Grandmother made 'finishing' me her pet project."

Katherine had rebelled against such an unloving atmosphere; certainly she must have known how Celie would fare. He relaxed his grip on the handle of the mug before he snapped it. "Why didn't your mother move out once she got back on her own feet?"

Celie toyed with the cookie while she considered his question. "She'd made one break and failed miserably. I'm not sure she found the commune to be all she expected. In those days, women still did the cooking and changed the diapers before they marched for peace and free love."

"What about your dad's parents?"

"They keep their distance."

More hurt bundled inside, he realized. Couldn't fate have given her at least one side of a loving family? He made himself swallow several gulps of coffee while he tamed his growing anger, speaking again only when he was certain he could keep his voice level. "I can't imagine my mother abandoning one of her grandchildren."

Celie shrugged. "It's just as well, I suppose. If they'd tried to stake a claim, Grandmother would have made a fuss."

"I take it she does that often?"

"Often and well. She goes right for the jugular." She glanced at his emptied mug. "Are you finished?"

"This being the nineties, I'll carry my own dishes to the sink," he said, but she picked it up anyhow. As she walked to the sink, Mark watched the robe hug her curves and contours, knowing her grandma would strike him dead if she could read the thoughts running rampant through his mind.

"They're playing Christmas movies on cable," Celie told him when she turned away from the sink.

That ran a sad second to what he really wanted to do. Still, he'd grovel for every moment he could spend alone with her. "Good. We need to get you into the Christmas spirit." He followed her into the living room and looked around at the room void of decoration. "Tomorrow I'm going to hang some mistletoe and holly."

"There's no need—"

"There certainly is. I'm going to banish the ghosts of Christmas past."

"There aren't any ghosts in my past, Christmas or otherwise."

He knew better than to argue. Picking up the remote control, he switched off the lamp before he sat beside her on the sofa. "Then we'll work on your Christmas future."

Flicking through the channels, he stopped at a colorized Christmas classic he'd seen a dozen times. "I should have decorated without mentioning it, so you'd be surprised."

She yawned. "I hate surprises."

The room was dark and cozy. A perfect time, he realized, to bring up the lettergram tucked in the bottom of his duffel. Rehearsing his opening lines, he cleared his throat and twisted to face her. The words died in his throat.

She slept, her head resting against the sofa back. In the dim light from the television screen he studied her face while he slipped an arm around her shoulders and drew her closer. Not waking, she snuggled against him.

Painful as it had been, letting her go earlier had been the best thing. Otherwise, he had the feeling, she'd have awakened in the morning hung over with guilt, more ready than ever to ship him off to the high seas. Instead, she'd lowered the barricade a bit more. Inch by inch, painstakingly slow, but he realized that would make what was soon to be his all the sweeter.

Celie trudged up the steps, surprised to see them shoveled free of snow. Not that it was any less than what she was beginning to expect from Mark. This morning, when a crisis call roused her and she'd alternately apologized and explained to him that no one else could help, he'd been understanding about postponing their museum trip.

For payback, she'd take him to dinner at Vera's. Vera seemed to approve of Mark wholeheartedly and would go out of her way to serve him something special. New England beef stew, Celie decided, pulling off her boots. While walking home, she had rehearsed an explanation for her impulsive behavior last night and planned to deliver it the moment she walked through the door.

In her living room, she stopped short and stared, letting the brief-case she carried thump onto the tug.

Miniature white bulbs circled the bay window and twinkled around the fireplace mirror, appearing to flicker in time with the holiday music wafting from the stereo speakers.

Her throat constricting at the emotion ripping through her, Celie headed toward the fireplace. The wedding angels she'd made a point of placing at the far ends of the mantel now rested in the middle, their wings properly entwined. On either side, impish ceramic elves dangled red felt stockings, her name cross-stitched on one, Mark's on the other.

In the mirror she saw Mark standing in the kitchen doorway. Watching her, he wiped his hands on a red-and-green-checked towel. "Welcome home," he said softly.

She should resent his disregarding her wishes and decorating her home behind her back, but she found it hopeless to pretend she felt anything but delighted. She couldn't stop smiling as she traced the name stitched on her stocking. "Don't tell me you sew, too?"

"My grandma made those for us. Mom sent a gift, too, but you can't open it until Christmas Day."

Why would his family shower her with gifts? She turned around to ask, but before she could, he flung the towel over his shoulder and bowed. "Your table is ready, madam."

"You didn't have to make dinner," she protested, hungry enough to be glad that he had. At the dining room door, he caught her by the shoulders and kissed her so quickly she didn't have time to push him away. Or wrap her arms around his neck and draw him close.

"Mistletoe," he murmured.

She saw it attached to the doorframe above her and tried to summon a disapproving frown. "That's not fair—"

"All's fair in love and war." He nudged her into the dining room.

He'd set the table using the gold-rimmed Limoges china she'd inherited from her great-grandmother. As long as Celie could remember, it had never been used, only showcased in the custom-designed display cabinet, always awaiting some special occasion. Tonight it seemed an appropriate part of the holiday decor.

After seating her, Mark lit two bayberry tapers nestled in the pine-cone centerpiece, then switched off the overhead light. Then he pulled a bottle of wine from the silver cooler on the breakfront and filled two crystal glasses. He handed her one and lifted the other. "To the best things in life," he toasted, touching his glass to hers.

She sipped her wine while he brought a tureen from the kitchen. When he uncovered it, she found the aroma so familiar she frowned. "You made this?"

"Of course not." He offered her a basket of crusty French bread. "I asked Vera what you'd order on a miserable day like today, and she sent me home with a pot of her beef stew. How was work?"

In between bites of bread and stew, Celie told him. She'd placed another battered child, then spent the rest of the day representing the shelter in an emergency meeting with local politicians. Winter funding had run short, and winter wasn't even half over.

When she finished talking, Mark said, "I hope you aren't too tired. Thought we'd pick out a tree after dinner."

She'd already given in gracefully on the decorations. Without saying so directly, she tried to refuse a tree. "You've done more than enough already."

Refilling her wineglass, he offered her a reassuring smile. "If that's your ecological conscience objecting, we can buy one of those artificial ones that will last the rest of our natural lives. I promise I'll hang every single ornament myself."

"Who's going to take them all down?"

"Who says you have to take them down? We'll start a new family tradition."

"I've suffered enough family traditions to last a lifetime." That she would even vaguely consider his suggestion proved she was overtired. "And I don't need a tree."

"You don't *want* a tree," he corrected. "Does it feel good playing Scrooge?"

"I don't see the sense of pretending in the magic of Christmas, or giving gifts to people you've ignored all year. Seems like buying penance at church in the Middle Ages to eliminate your sins to date, then heading out the door to commit a few more."

He weighed her words before he spoke. "Most people see Christmas as a bridge between their grown-up and childhood days.

"I wouldn't know about most people," she said, hating her brittle voice. He waited, watching her, but she had nothing more to say. To prove it, she stood and began stacking the dishes.

Mark stopped her. "I pulled KP tonight. I take it you didn't lug that briefcase home just to impress me?"

"I have files to review before a court hearing tomorrow."

He leaned across the chair and kissed her. Before she could protest, he pointed to the mistletoe strung around the base of the pewter chandelier. "There's plenty more where that came from. Shall I show you all the places it's hanging?"

She shook her head. "I have a feeling you'd do more than just *show* me."

She waited until his hands were filled with dishes before she ventured through the mistletoe-strung doorway. In the living room, she slipped off her suit coat and retrieved her briefcase. Sitting on the floor, she opened a manila folder and began making notes, trying to ignore Mark as he bustled around the kitchen whistling snatches of the carol Barbra Streisand crooned through the speakers. Pleasant as it sounded, Celie knew she wouldn't get anything done with his cheerful distraction.

As if he read her mind, he appeared in the kitchen doorway. "What can I do to help?"

She calculated the length of time she needed to finish her work. "Give me two hours' peace and quiet. Shannon keeps a pile of best-sellers on a shelf in her bedroom, if you like horror—"

"I don't intend to waste my holiday leave reading Stephen King," Mark said good-naturedly. "If you're so determined to get rid of me, lend me your car keys. I'd like to see Boston by night."

After he left, she switched off the CD player. The quiet seemed louder than she remembered, so she turned it on again, lowering the volume before she sat down and tackled the first folder.

Two hours later she stretched her arms over her head and yawned. The late hours she'd kept the night before were beginning to take their toll. Scooting back against the sofa, she rested her head against the seat cushions and closed her eyes, promising herself if Mark didn't come in thirty minutes she'd go upstairs and call it a day.

Half asleep, she jumped, startled, when she heard scratching on the foyer door. When she opened it she faced a sea of bobbing green needles.

"Care to lend a hand?" Mark's voice was muffled by pine branches. "I think it's stuck in the doorway."

"Serves you right," she said, trying not to sound as foolishly pleased as she felt. "I told you I didn't want a tree."

"It's not for you, it's for me. I needed a place to pile your presents." When she didn't answer, he poked his hands through the branches, separating two so he could see her. "Just help me get it through the door and you won't have to do another thing, I swear. I'll put it up, decorate it, take it down. Scout's honor."

She considered. "I don't suppose you can take it back?"

"All sales final. If you could just grab the end . . ."

She did, tugging the branches inch by inch through the doorway while Mark maneuvered from the other side until the tree was sprawled on the living room rug.

Celie planted her hands on her hips and studied the tree with a critical eye. It looked as if it would fill half the living room. "You couldn't find a smaller one?"

"This one looked small in the lot. Where do you want it?"

It would be perfect standing before the bay window, she thought with more excitement than she should feel for a tree she didn't want. "This was your idea. You decide."

Mark wiped sap from his hands onto his jeans while he surveyed the room. "In front of the bay window. If you could just get that shopping bag I left in the foyer . . ."

When she did, he rummaged through it and pulled out a box

holding a metal tree stand. He eyed the ceiling as he loosened the screws to the stand. "How tall?"

"Ten feet."

"Thought so. This tree's about nine, I think; should be a perfect fit." He hoisted it, then grunted. "Might be a little easier if you slip the holder onto the bottom."

He'd promised to do everything himself, but it seemed rather inappropriate to argue the point while he sagged under the weight of the pine. She positioned the holder and tightened the screws. "Done."

Mark exhaled as he set the tree on the floor, then frowned at the topmost branch brushing the ceiling. "We won't have room for the star. Got a hacksaw?"

Celie shook her head. "We could skip the star."

"Not on your life. Meat cleaver? Switchblade? You must have something I can use to take a few inches from the bottom."

"You could cut a few inches from the top, since those branches aren't very thick. Scissors would probably work."

"You always shorten a Christmas tree from the bottom," he told her. "It's bad luck to whack away the green."

"You're superstitious?"

"I'm not one to tempt the fates. Since I can't impress you with sheer charm, I've developed a new respect for outside forces, good or evil."

"I'll trim them, then." She found the scissors in the kitchen and snipped several inches from the top, then helped him walk the tree to a spot in front of the bay window.

Against her better judgment, she resumed the topic he'd started. "You're old enough to know wishing on stars doesn't work," she said, ripping open a package of tree lights.

"Sure it does." He squatted to arrange a glitter-covered white drop cloth over the tree holder. "Haven't you ever wanted something so badly you could taste it? Something that keeps you awake nights making ridiculous promises you swear to keep if your wish were granted?"

Silly as it sounded, she knew exactly what he meant. "After we moved to Hargrave Manor, I promised my mother I'd be good the rest of my life if we'd just move back to our own house. Turned out to be a waste of breath."

Watching her, he rocked back on his heels. "Ever since the morning we met, I've wished for the same thing over and over."

She refused to look up from the string of lights she was trying to untangle. She wanted to say she didn't care, that his dreams were none of her business, but she knew it wouldn't be true.

"I want to start and end each day looking at you, saying I love you, listening to you say the same to me." Standing, he crossed the room and captured her hands before she found the presence of mind to pull away. The string of lights tumbled to the floor. "Too much to ask for, maybe," he said, his voice low.

"Maybe not," she whispered.

"That's not quite the unqualified answer I've waited to hear."

She tried to smile at the frustrated look on his face, but she couldn't. "I won't lie to you, Mark. We seem compatible, and I think we could have a satisfying marriage. But I won't stand here and say 'I love you' when I don't."

He let her go. "I'm willing to wait."

Retrieving the cord of lights, she spied a sprig of mistletoe tacked above the bay window. She stared at it, then at Mark. Even though he didn't touch her, her body reacted as if he had.

His eyes darkened, telling her he'd been as aware of her reaction as she, but he moved out of reach, stepping closer to the tree before he spoke. "Hand me that box of ornaments, will you?"

It was only a temporary reprieve, but she was grateful for the chance to regroup her senses. Once they were finished with the tree, they could sit down and she would present her excuses for her behavior last night.

Despite his earlier promise to hang the decorations himself, she soon found herself doing half the work. She reminded him of such when they finally finished.

"I'm a born delegator," he said, crossing the room to turn off the light. He walked back and stood by her side to admire their handiwork.

Around her, the cozy darkness was punctuated by a rainbow of miniature flashing lights. Well worth the trouble, she had to admit.

"Probably not as grand as the Hargrave family tree," Mark said, "But I think it looks pretty good."

"It's beautiful," Celie corrected, trying to ignore the ache settling in her breastbone. She found it strange to miss something she'd never had. "We don't put up a tree at home, except for the one in the ballroom, just for show."

Without looking, she could feel him staring at her in the subdued light. "You never had a tree?"

"Not at the commune; I suppose they considered it too commercial. When we moved back to Boston, Grandmother didn't feel it appropriate to celebrate while my mother was in mourning. It just became habit, I guess, decorating with candles and holly instead of bothering with everything else."

"Are you sorry you *bothered* tonight?"

"No." Dismayed to feel tears pricking her eyes, she tried to blink them away before he noticed. How could she make a fool of herself over a dead tree? "I suppose next you'll be baking fruitcake."

"If that's what it takes to make you happy." He brushed a tear from her cheek.

Unwilling to subdue the pleasure dancing under her skin, she closed her fingers around his wrist and kept his hand against her face. Overwhelmed by his closeness, the intimate glow of the lights, the heady scent of pine swirling around her, she shut her eyes, surprised the combination of moonlight and wine she'd blamed aboard ship hadn't been nearly as intoxicating.

Lifting her head when he drew her against him, she let him kiss away the tears she couldn't for the life of her stop.

"What do you want, Celie?" he whispered, his breath bouncing against her damp cheek.

"I don't know." A welter of emotions scrambled what little rational thought she still possessed. "I know what I *don't* want, and that's someone trampling through my life, rearranging my priorities."

He smoothed her hair. "I'm not trying to rearrange—"

"Yes, you are. You know how I feel about Christmas and you brought all these things into my home anyhow."

"I want to make you happy," he said, his hands stilling.

"You're making me cry."

He hugged her closer and cradled her in his arms. "I'll take down the decorations, get rid of the tree tomorrow. I promise."

"Don't you dare." Tears choked her voice.

"I'll even pack and leave tonight, if that's what you want."

She panicked, her arms tightening around his back. "I don't know what I want." She spoke the truth, although she knew whatever she wanted, she wanted him be part of it. She looked into his eyes, which could see deeper into her soul more than she could. "Except that I want you."

That much he knew, she told herself. He'd known it from the instant they'd smiled at each other across the dawnlit deck, the first night they'd kissed, wrapped in a cocoon of sea-misted moonlight, the morning they'd reluctantly parted outside his base.

Since then the want had intensified ten-fold, a hundred-fold,

magnified by something more essential. In case he didn't know,
she told him. "I need you."

The words she'd never before found necessary to say floated
effortlessly from her throat. Not at all what he wanted to hear, she
knew, but it was the most at the moment she could give. She tensed,
waiting for him to tell her it wasn't enough.

"It's a start," he murmured, the gruffness in his voice indicating
he realized how much it had cost her to make the admission. Burying his head in her hair, he nuzzled it out of the way to sample the
skin on the nape of her neck. "We're making progress," he said
when she snuggled closer.

He kissed her temples, her forehead, her nose, playful and teasing, murmuring her name over and over. But when he finally
reached her mouth, he kissed her as if he were famished, as if he'd
never get enough. His hands swept down her back, molding her
close to him, but not close enough he couldn't fill his palms with
her breasts, touching, shaping, stroking them through the silk of
her blouse until she moaned.

"Who in the world designed these?" he muttered, fumbling with
the seeded pearl buttons.

"Ralph Lauren."

He caught her laughter in his mouth when she pushed his hands
away and unfastened her blouse herself. Her mouth felt like hot
velvet to his exploring tongue, its sweetness inviting him to sample
her passion, taunting him with promises of pleasures yet to come.
And even if that promise didn't yet come with heart and soul attached, he would take what he could and pray the rest would follow.
For the time, it was all he deserved. All he needed.

Only it wasn't. Aroused to a sustained ache, his body warred
with his mind even as he gentled the kiss and tried to button her
blouse. Through the shadows cloaking her face, he could see the
bewilderment in her eyes.

"I'm sorry," he whispered. "I didn't mean to take advantage of
the situation."

"The situation," she echoed blankly.

His fingers suddenly clumsy, he hadn't managed to secure a
single button. He finally gave up, letting his hands drop to his
sides, watching her clutch the wrinkled silk together as she watched
and waited for him to explain.

When he didn't, she took a defensive step backward. "I thought
you wanted—"

"What I want has nothing to do with it." He curled his hands into fists to keep from touching her. "I didn't hightail it to Boston to find a little fun for the holidays."

"I understand—"

She gave him a dazzling confident smile, one he hadn't seen since he'd first stepped back into her life, one he now knew she wore to hide her feelings. One that confirmed his feeling that he was stating his case very badly.

Maybe there was nothing he could say to make her understand, but he tried anyhow. "I love you."

"Yes, so you've said."

He wanted to kiss away the wintry hurt from her voice, make her heated again with reckless passion. Instead, he continued attempting to explain. "I'm not good at compromising. I want it all."

Or nothing. He intended on finishing the ultimatum, but his mouth refused to utter the blatant lie.

He couldn't settle for nothing. In fact, he'd settle for whatever she offered.

He wanted to demand she tell him she loved him. But the words had to come from her willingly, not released by passion or threats, but by the same sheer intensity he experienced, one that would be magnified merely by being reciprocated.

She understood exactly what he meant, he saw by the way her eyes and false smile apologized for what she wouldn't say. By rights he should coax her back into his arms and soothe away the pain he'd inflicted. However, he knew as she walked up the stairs without looking back, that would be only a temporary solution.

He intended on playing for keeps.

Nine

Without opening her eyes, Celie fumbled to quiet the snooze alarm. She felt she hadn't slept at all, but in fact the moment her head hit the pillow the night before, she'd slipped into fitful dreams, erotic fantasies tangled with domestic ones.

After climbing out of bed, she stumbled into the shower. Ten minutes later, while finger-drying her hair under the heat lamp, she stared at her reflection in the mirror. Nothing on her face reflected the turmoil inside gnawing at her heart.

She figured Mark would still be asleep since it wasn't yet six o'clock, so she eased the bathroom door open and tiptoed into the hall. She made a face as she heard the clattering of pans below accompanied by a cheerfully whistled "White Christmas."

Even as she contemplated dressing and slipping unnoticed out the front door, a board squeaked beneath her feet. Hoping he hadn't heard, she stopped a moment.

"Breakfast is ready," he called.

She wasn't ready to face herself, let alone him. "I'm not really hungry."

"I'm going to serve you in bed," he said, as if he hadn't heard her.

He sounded determined to get his way, and she didn't have enough energy this morning to fight him. "I'm already up," she said, scrambling down the stairs. She found it impossible to walk through the living room without looking at the tree. Mark had plugged in the lights, and they twinkled cheerfully as she passed. As she neared the kitchen, the scent of pine mingled with that of cinnamon.

Mark met her at the doorway. Her pulse quickening at his smile, she raised her eyebrows at the plate of sweet rolls that sat in the middle of the kitchen table. "Been baking?"

He handed her a cup of tea. "Vera dropped them by this morning. They're still warm."

She started to ask how he'd convinced Vera to agree to such an ungodly hour for delivery, but then thought better of it. She had more than enough to worry about already.

She sat and pulled one of the rolls apart from the others, and found it was all she could do to keep from groaning when she sank her teeth into it. Extra cinnamon, extra icing, fresh from the oven—the only way a cinnamon roll should be.

Mark sat down across from her with a mug of coffee. "I didn't realize Vera was one of your clients. The very first, she says."

Celie nodded. "One of the center's success stories. Her husband worked odd jobs all his life and never filed for social security withholding. After he died, she literally had nothing left except her pride. When she came to the center, she wouldn't let us help unless she could do something in return. What she could do was cook and bake."

Knowing it wasn't polite to tear into a second roll when he hadn't yet had his first, Celie reached for her tea instead. "She went to work in the center's kitchen, but she had a dream of opening a diner, even took night courses in business management to prove it at the community college. The center offered her their first interest-free loan."

"Which you cosigned." After selecting one for himself, Mark pushed the plate of rolls closer to Celie. "She doesn't talk about the center helping her half as much as she talks about you."

She didn't want to know what stories—true or false—Vera had been sharing. No doubt they were mixed with a liberal dose of matchmaking. "Shouldn't believe everything you hear. What are you doing today?"

"Going to lunch with Charlie Coffey. He still thinks he can talk me into drumming up funds for his campaign. Figured I'd let him talk while he shows me around the city."

"That's a pretty steep price to pay for sight-seeing," Celie pointed out.

"If you'd take the day off, I'd cancel my interview so we could sit down and learn everything there is to know about each other. Exchange growing-up stories and the like."

She reluctantly decided against eating a third roll. "I'm too old for show-and-tell."

"At lunch yesterday, Charlie told me some things—"

"Lunch with Charlie? Yesterday?" Last night it hadn't occurred to her to ask Mark if he'd done anything that day besides decorating her home. Knowing it might be best to change the subject, she tried to think of another topic, but the glint lighting his eyes worried her. "What kind of things?"

Grinning, Mark tore apart the last roll and offered her half. "About your replacing your family's coat-of-arms flag with a Jolly Roger."

"I was only ten," she said, surprised to find herself on the defensive. "We'd done a family tree for history class, and I found a pirate way back. Grandmother was horrified that I'd mentioned him in my report." Celie couldn't help but smile now, remembering the uproar over something so trivial.

"The newspaper sent out a reporter to photograph the flag and get a statement . . ." She stopped and narrowed her eyes. Mark's laugh, she had a feeling, was not in reference to the flag. "What?"

"I got the impression you grew up prim and proper. In fact, you gave me that impression yourself."

"I'd hardly call switching flags a rebellious act."

"How about the time you climbed onto an oak outside your bedroom window after watching *Pollyanna?*"

She'd been stuck in the tree all night, as terrified of falling as of waking her grandmother. The next morning the fire company had to rescue her using a ladder truck, providing another photo opportunity for the local news media, followed by a stern threat of boarding school. That ended her streak of adventure then and there.

There were a dozen other escapades he could have been told about, and she didn't care to hear any more. "You must have been bored out of your socks yesterday, if all Charlie talked about was me."

"The poor man claims he started out in life shy and introverted until you took him under your wing."

She laughed. "Amazing how politicians weave fiction with truth."

"Says the worst day in his life was when you handed back his engagement ring." Mark's tone shifted from teasing to something she couldn't quite recognize, something that darkened his eyes.

Jealousy? she wondered. If so, it was unwarranted. "We weren't in love, even though we tried to be. There just wasn't any . . ." She paused, trying to find the correct word to describe what she'd found lacking. "Passion. Maybe because I knew him too well, since we'd grown up together."

"Maybe he just wasn't the man for you."

No maybe about it. A teenager at the time, she'd latched on to Charlie's proposal, viewing it as an easy escape route from her grandmother's clutches. Her regret over her hasty agreement was appeased by the fact that he'd been more concerned about marrying into another prestigious family than marrying for love. "His heart healed soon enough," she pointed out. "A few months later he'd proposed to someone else."

"Any regrets?"

Surprised by the sudden tension in his voice, she shook her head. "He's devoted to his career. I'm sure by now we'd have gone separate ways."

She saw his shoulders relax as he considered her words. He finished his coffee before he spoke again. "Let's go outside and watch the sun rise."

"It won't come for another hour or so." Celie stood and carried her cup to the sink. "Besides, I've got to get ready for work."

She rinsed the traces of icing from her fingers and, when she turned off the water, realized he stood directly behind her. "You're under the mistletoe again," he murmured.

She heard her robe whisper against his jeans, then felt his hands on her waist. Sensation blanketed her mind, making his mouth nibbling her neck the center of her consciousness. His fingertips glided over her ribs until her breasts hovered above his palms, thrusting for his touch under two layers of flannel.

"About last night," he whispered. "I should have accepted you on your own terms."

Her pulse thudded in the hollow of her throat. "I don't know what my terms are anymore," she confessed shakily.

The robe, the one she'd chosen because it looked so sensible and safe hanging in her closet, did nothing to hide his reaction to her. She didn't resist the irresistible compulsion to press against him.

"This is in the way." He undid the knot on her fabric belt.

Her senses were slipping out of her control, but she made no effort to harness them, perfectly content to close her eyes and revel in the pleasure she felt when he parted the robe and pushed it from her shoulders. As he cupped her breasts, she felt his breath explode, hot in the hollow behind her ear.

Turning her head, she found his mouth. Coffee, she tasted, as his lips moved on hers, and cinnamon. Still cocooned beneath the nightgown, her body ached for a more personal touch.

His hands raced over her gown, heating her skin underneath while he explored her mouth lazily and thoroughly, as if he had all the time in the world to learn its secrets. "You're going to be late for work," he whispered.

"I'll stay later, make up the time tonight." She turned to face him, ready to absorb the strength of his body against hers, to intensify the pleasure his mouth and hands were inciting.

"I love you," she whispered, confident in the words and the overwhelming meaning behind them. The thought of spending the rest of her life at his side suddenly seemed so right she couldn't imagine anything else.

"I know," he said, his arms tightening around her. "I don't have much, Celie. All I can offer you is what I'd vow before a preacher— for better, for worse, for sicker, for poorer."

She smiled at him. "Who could ask for anything more?"

He answered with a kiss.

She felt cool air sweep across her shoulders when he unbuttoned her nightgown. His hands danced over her ribs. Shaken by the sensations his questing fingers aroused, she closed her eyes when they splayed, warm and strong, over her breasts. Pressing her mouth to his throat, she felt his heartbeat hammering in time with her own.

"I think we'd better wait."

At his hoarse protest, she jerked her head back. "What?"

Closing his eyes, Mark rested his forehead against hers. "If we're going to do this, we're going to do it right."

"We're doing just fine." She wrapped her arms around his neck and tried to pull him close again.

"Except that you'll be running off to work soon."

She tried not to groan. He was right. For the moment, though, she clung to him, not wanting to leave. "This is getting to be a habit."

"Anticipation is half the fun." He smoothed her gown back into place, his fingers lingering at her open collar to trace the V of flushed skin it revealed. "For dinner, bring home a loaf of bread and a jug of wine. That's all we need."

"Hold the thought." She stood on tiptoe for one last kiss.

Mark stepped from the limousine and stared at the Hargrave mansion. Beneath the leaden winter sky, its stark lines rose, as forbidding and hard as he imagined Celie's grandma could be. The sight of a century-old oak towering at the side of the house made him smile, for a moment causing him to forget his apprehension about the invitation he'd received an hour ago.

The uniformed driver standing next to him checked his watch. "Madam's expecting you at noon, sir. It's now eleven fifty-six."

Mark nodded, then strode up the wide stone steps. Before he could lift the brass boar's-head knocker, the door swung open. A butler ushered him inside, then bowed as he accepted his coat. "Madam is waiting in the dining room, sir."

Mark felt like a ten-year-old heading toward the principal's office as he followed the uniformed man down the dark-wooded hallway. After escorting him into the dining room, the butler slipped away.

"Sit down, Mr. Edwards." Grace Hargrave's steely voice made the invitation a command.

Only two settings had been placed on the table, erasing his hope that Louise might put in a good word or two. "Good afternoon, Mrs. Hargrave." He refused to let his voice reflect the stirring of unease he felt.

Not returning his smile, she motioned him to a chair, then rang a bell to summon the maid. She didn't speak again until the maid placed two bowls of soup on the table and disappeared.

He couldn't help notice the surprise flickering over Grace's face when he unfolded the linen napkin and placed it on his lap, then chose the soup spoon from the elaborate silverware setting. He silently thanked his Annapolis polish.

"I'd be insulting your intelligence if I pretended this was a social invitation," he said quietly. "Why don't you come right to the point?"

"I asked a private investigator to check up on you. He says you're courting my granddaughter."

"I am." After tasting the soup, he found it too rich and too bland. Placing the spoon down, he toyed with requesting a sizzling steak cooked rare but figured the conversation would end before the meat hit the grill.

"I want it stopped."

He resisted a childish impulse to pick up the spoon, slam it into the soup, and splatter buttery broth over the snow-white tablecloth. Instead, he smiled politely and looked her square in the eye. "I appreciate your interest in the matter, but Celie is old enough to make her own decisions."

Grace's faded eyes narrowed. "I'm sure you've learned her trust fund becomes active the day she turns thirty."

"Two days after Christmas." He knew about her birthday, but not about her trust fund. He also knew Grace would never believe him if he told her.

"Then you're aware certain stipulations are involved, one being her money cannot be inherited by a spouse. In death or divorce, the balance reverts back to the family or passes to her children. Of course, while the spouse is alive, there is no restriction on how the money is spent."

The insinuation was explicit enough to make his skin crawl, and he fought to keep his temper in check. "I'm not after Celie's money."

"True love, I suppose?"

Although the words dripped with derision, he refused to rise to the bait. Refolding his napkin, he placed it on the table, then stood and pushed in his chair. "You'll have to excuse me, Mrs. Hargrave. I'm not hungry after all."

"Sit down, young man." The woman's jaw jutted when he remained standing. "I took the liberty of having you investigated."

He bit back a rude comment. "That must have been a waste of money."

"You do have a rather unimpressive past. An arrest for a bar fight—"

"I was nineteen."

"And three traffic tickets. Then again, it's easy to conceal unsavory acts. I've been compelled to resort to that myself occasionally to protect the family name."

He forced himself to stand at military ease, his hands behind his back. "The point, Mrs. Hargrave?"

"Bring me that folder on the sideboard."

He did, feeling as if he'd handed her a loaded weapon.

She extracted a sheaf of papers and thumbed, through them. "Your parents own a farm in Arizona."

"Chinchilla ranch," he corrected, trying to second-guess the point of her observation. Nothing came to mind.

"Financially unstable, in the red for the past two years. The Western River Bank is foreclosing on the property if obligations aren't satisfied by the end of the month."

The same property he soon hoped to turn into a tax-free experimental energy farm. If she asked, he'd tell her.

"I appreciate a sense of family loyalty." She tapped her gnarled fingers against the folder. "Because I do, I believe I understand your seeking capital in such an unethical manner."

While he hadn't yet received final approval on his application for a federal grant, he had no reason to expect he wouldn't. Apparently her investigator hadn't done a thorough job, since she assumed he'd need to dip into Celie's trust fund to finance his future. "I'm not—"

"Tell me how much you need." She spoke as if he hadn't interrupted. "I'll wire your father the money within the hour.

Fighting the urge to wring her wrinkled neck, Mark grasped at the slim chance he'd misunderstood. "A loan?"

Her eyes said she wasn't fooled by his play of ignorance. "A bribe, Mr. Edwards. I'll solve your problem, you solve mine."

He laced his fingers together. "How's that?"

"In exchange for satisfying your family debt, I expect you to report to the airport tomorrow at noon, alone. My jet is at your disposal; Cecilia is not."

His patience spent, Mark walked to the head of the table. "At the risk of easing your suspicious mind, I fell in love with Celie before I knew she owned a dime. My feelings toward her would be the same whether she were an heiress or an orphaned bag lady. At the moment, I can't help imagining she'd be better off being the latter."

Grace's thin smile lacked even a trace of warmth. "You have twenty-four hours to consider the offer. I prefer not to involve Cecilia, but if you leave me no recourse, I'll be forced to expose you for the scoundrel you are."

He had plenty more to say but knew better than to waste his

breath. Spinning on his heel, he left the room, successfully fighting an impulse not to slam the door behind him.

He'd explain the situation to Celie over dinner, he decided as he pulled off his overcoat. He'd tell her how he'd convinced his brothers to lend him the money needed to match the federal grant dollar-for-dollar, how Charlie had promised to walk his application through the appropriate committee. If all went well, he'd hold the deed to the ranch by the end of the month. Of course, everything depended on her agreement to move to Arizona after they were married.

He'd ask her tonight, although first he'd tell her about the lettergram. At the moment, her grandma's threat didn't warrant mention. He would prove his intentions were honorable to the one woman who really mattered.

Sitting cross-legged on the sofa, Celie looked up when he strode into the living room. "How was lunch?"

She'd caught him off guard, since he hadn't expected to find her home this early in the day. Her smile distracted him, made him forget all his best intentions. "Something more pressing came up." He couldn't begin to tell her what, not with a dozen unkind adjectives poised on the top of his tongue to describe her grandmother.

"Thanks for the flowers and candy," Celie said, her smile widening.

He stared at her blankly for a moment before he remembered that he'd had a dozen roses and a tin of imported chocolates delivered to her office. "Just catching up on those dating rituals we missed," he told her, wondering how to ease into the subject of the lettergram.

Sitting beside her, he looked at the photo album she held. "What are you doing?"

She tapped a laminated page. "I wanted to show you a few photos of the *introvert* you met for lunch."

"I didn't—" He caught himself from admitting he hadn't eaten lunch with Charlie, realizing that would only open the floor for questions he wasn't yet fully prepared to answer. After taking the book, he leafed through pages of photographs capturing Charlie's antics on prints. Charlie and Celie dressed in country-western gear for Halloween. Side by side, posing at the debutante ball. Sitting astride quarter horses. Standing in front of the Eiffel Tower.

He couldn't tame the jealousy spearing through him. "Any pictures of you without him?"

She flipped to the front of the album to show the snapshots no doubt taken by proud parents. Some off center, some out of focus, all of them radiated love and warmth. Celie the chubby baby splashing in the bathtub. Celie the toddler standing next to her mother in a field of wildflowers.

He studied Katherine's faded image, her hair long and straight under a crown of daisies, her face catching the sunlight. "Your dad didn't have a chance, did he? She's as pretty then as you are now."

" 'Love at first sight,' " she always said." Celie smoothed her fingers over the picture. "Come to think of it, that's what Aunt Louise always says about her husband, too."

"Wise women, both of them." He traced a vein in Celie's wrist as she turned the pages. "Have a picture of your dad?"

Mark examined the black-and-white photograph she pointed to, of a man dressed in Army fatigues. Despite her startling resemblance to her mother, Mark could see traces of Celie in the lanky teenager's face.

"Last time I saw him, I was almost six," Celie said. "He must have been about twenty-five. I remember standing at the train station waving good-bye and wondering why my mother was crying. It never occurred to me he might not come home alive. Sometimes I wonder how different life would have been if . . ."

Her eyes glistening with tears, she looked at Mark and blinked them away. "Then again, I wouldn't have met you."

"Yes, you would." He had no doubts. "Destiny," he reminded her, pushing aside the album to draw her into his arms. "Are you home to stay today, or is the phone going to ring in the middle of an inopportune moment and summon you away?"

Shifting position, she rested her cheek against his chest. "I traded schedules, so someone else is on call today. As a matter of fact, I'm on vacation for the rest of the week. We'll take the phone off the hook."

Her fingers strayed from his collar to his belt buckle. He stilled her hand with his own before she could make him forget his resolve to clear up certain matters. "I said we're going to do things right this time. For dinner, I made reservations at that place Shannon recommended."

"Cancel them." She turned just enough to press her breasts against his chest.

He hauled her up in a less-disturbing position, kissing her soundly before he pushed her off his lap. "You're not fighting fair, woman."

"You told me yourself all's fair in love and war."

He couldn't resist kissing away her pout. "We have a few things to talk about first."

"A hundred things," she corrected. "Let's start with children."

"I think we'd better get married first. Love, honor, cherish, marry a woman, and children will follow. My father told me so when I was a teenager."

Celie grinned. "Beautiful thoughts, but he omitted an elementary part of the biological process."

"You'll have to show me later." He could put the cards on the table, tell her now, skip the restaurant altogether. Who needed a violinist and candlelit atmosphere to set the mood, anyhow?

She slid her fingers over his jaw, up to his temple. "You have silver hair."

"Consequences of the long wait I've endured. I felt myself growing more ancient by the minute waiting for you to realize we belonged together. What are you doing?"

It seemed to strike her funny that he asked a question when the answer was so obvious. "Unbuttoning your shirt."

Her hands slipped through the opening, cool against his chest, making it difficult for him to draw a breath. She buried her face in his shoulder. "Thought we'd kill a few hours before dinnertime," she whispered, nuzzling the skin she'd exposed.

His determination to confess the lettergram misunderstanding wavered when she finger-counted his ribs. He caught her wrist and pulled it to his face, kissing her open palm. "We'll kill it like two sensible adults."

"I thought that's what we were doing."

This time, after he kissed away her pout, he stood and moved out of reach. He needed to call Charlie again to check on the progress of his grant application. Under normal circumstances, he'd work with the system, but Grace Hargrave had imposed an unexpected deadline. Knowing people tended to misinterpret one-sided conversations, he needed to make his call from a pay phone. And he still hadn't found Celie a gift.

When he came back, he'd handle the other things—the lettergram, the proposal he'd been rehearsing since breakfast. Once he tended to all those little things, he planned to spend the next twenty-four hours or so making up for the three precious weeks they'd lost.

"I'm going out for a few hours. I have some last-minute shopping to do," he told her. "Any gift suggestions?

She scrambled off the couch and followed him into the foyer. "I have everything I need," she reminded him, watching him pull on his coat.

He kissed her forehead. "I'll be back in an hour or two."

After he left, Celie went upstairs. It had been months since she'd gone out for dinner—a real dinner date, not merely a function to pitch a plea for funding the center. She felt jittery as a schoolgirl, although she couldn't help wondering whether that could be attributed to what would come *after* dinner.

Undressing, she gathered her hair into a twist and pinned it atop her head. She sloshed a liberal dose of bubble-bath crystals into the tub, then let the bathwater run full-blast, nearly filling the tub before she climbed in and let the silky warmth slide over her.

Mark certainly was right about anticipation. She'd been a useless pile of nerves at work, staring at the same file for an hour while she fantasized about the evening ahead.

Those same fantasies whirled around her mind now. Closing her eyes, she leaned her head against the back of the tub.

A knock on the door roused her.

"I'm in the tub," she called, scrunching under the cooling cover of bubbles when Mark opened the door.

He walked into the bathroom. "Didn't you hear me calling? I thought you'd left—"

Instead of completing his sentence he stared at her face, at her shoulders, until her skin tingled as if he'd touched her. After pulling her towel from the rack, he snapped it open. "It's almost four-thirty; our early dinner reservations are for five."

"I'm nearly finished." Her voice faltered as he bent to kiss her hair. When his breath brushed her wet skin and cooled it, she shivered, although she felt a rush of heat deep inside.

He kissed her shoulder. "You smell good."

"Something Shannon picked up in Paris for my birthday. I'll be dry and dressed in no time," she promised, her voice as breathless as his.

"I don' think so." Dropping the towel to the floor, he knelt beside the tub.

She felt her hair tumbling free from its twist. When she reached to push it back in place, he caught her wrist, moving it out of the way to drop a dew-light kiss on her mouth. Her hair fell over his hand as he cradled her neck and kissed her again.

Drowning in sensation, she gripped the edge of the tub when his mouth found her throat. The openmouthed kiss seared her skin. When his hands dipped beneath the water, her breasts surged against them, her nipples jutting against his palms. A current of pleasure jagged through her as he slid one hand down her back, letting his fingers explore each vertebra.

Not until she clutched his arms did she realize he still wore his shirt. "You're getting wet," she said, her whisper fading to a moan when his fingers brushed her inner thighs.

"You're getting out." He drew her to her feet, scooping up the towel and wrapping it around her while he kissed her again.

Undoing the buttons to his shirt, she pushed it from his shoulders, her mouth following her fingers as they glided over his hair-roughened skin. Searching out the shadowed hollow of his throat, she whispered his name, then moved to explore the taut muscled flesh below. Beneath her lips she felt his heart racing in wild pace with her own.

She realized the towel had dropped, felt cool air brush her skin before his lips trailed over her throat and mapped a path to her breasts. When he drew a nipple into his mouth and teased it into a throbbing peak, the pleasure rippling through her buckled her knees. Encircling his neck with her arms, she clung to him as his probing touch stole away her breath.

His hands pressed against the small of her back, and she swayed against him, feeling him hot and hard against her thigh. "We'll miss dinner," he warned, his hands drifting over her hips.

She danced her fingers through the arrow of hair down his taut stomach, stopping for a moment at his belt. "We can eat after . . ."

Instead of finishing her sentence she cupped him with both hands, feeling his pulsing need and savoring the shudder she felt rock him while she worked his belt's buckle loose.

Finally she melted against his bare skin and ran her hands over his back, down his hips, returning touch for touch, kiss for kiss, taste for taste. Shifting her legs, she rocked against him, feeling his muscles grow rigid beneath her fingers.

He pushed her tangled hair out of the way to nip her earlobe. "It would be a shame to waste that antique bed of yours."

He swung her into his arms, and she buried her face in the curve of his neck as he strode to the bedroom. "You swept me off my feet before," she whispered shakily.

When she felt herself falling onto the bed, she kept her arms locked around his neck so he followed, his weight pinning her to the mattress. Like velvet-encased steel, his fullness pressed against her, and she slid her hands down his back, urging his hips against hers, parting her legs to cradle him between her thighs.

Tucking her legs around his waist, he entered her slowly, watching her eyes darken in the late-afternoon shadows, ignoring the bite of her fingers against his knotted muscles.

She could feel the tension holding his muscles rigid when she tightened her legs around him to urge him closer. Cherishing the pleasure spiraling through her at his welcomed invasion, she shuddered at the need that tore at her.

"Mark," she whispered, clutching him. She felt as if she'd shatter into a million pieces, and before she did, she needed to tell him once more. "I love you."

His hand slid between them to the apex of her thighs, rushing her to an ultimate release, a fevered blinding pleasure beyond thought, beyond reason, which left her gasping for breath while tremors racked her body. Moaning her name against her flushed skin, he joined her.

Stunned, she buried her face in the hollow of his neck. Like a narcotic, she thought, trying to restore the breath crushed from her lungs when he collapsed atop her, love could be drugging, intense, addicting.

"You're mine," he whispered as he stroked her damp skin and soothed the quivery muscles underneath with feathery kisses.

He spoke the truth. She knew she no longer had a heart of her own. He'd taken possession of it but had given her his own in return.

"I'm yours," she agreed, letting him fit her body against his. Too weary to even rearrange the quilt wadded beneath them, she nestled close, tasting salt on his skin when she kissed him. "I love you."

"I know." A moment later, he slept. She could tell by his even breathing stirring her hair, hair no doubt still damp and hopelessly tangled. Yet she stayed awake, suspended in passion's afterglow, and listened to his heart beating steadily against her cheek.

Ten

Sitting beside Mark, Celie studied him in the last traces of daylight. Limbs askew, he possessed more than his share of the double bed. A small price to pay for letting him into her life, she decided. Letting her hair tumble over his shoulders, she whispered his name until he opened his eyes, then kissed his breastbone before she spoke. "I think we've blown our dinner reservations. Should I call and make new ones?"

"Just give me a few more minutes." Wrapping her in his embrace, he closed his eyes again.

Her fingers drifted over his stomach, dragged across his inner thighs. "I'm going to finish my bath."

Kicking away the sheet tangled around his ankles, Mark tightened his hold. "Don't waste your time—we aren't done yet."

"I look a mess," she protested, although she allowed him to kiss her.

"You look well-loved." He smiled at her. "Is it too late to plan a Christmas wedding?"

Her tongue drew a lazy path along his shoulder. "I'd say so, since tomorrow is Christmas Eve."

"If we file the papers tomorrow, we could be married on your birthday. Justice of the peace?"

She lifted her head and stared at him. "You're serious?"

"Scout's honor." Catching her hand, he traced it over his heart. "If you think I'm going to leave you unhitched, prey to every leering bachelor in Boston—"

Still, she had to be pragmatic. "You have to leave, whether we're married or not."

"I'd go AWOL first. You could represent me in military court, prove I was insane. Crime of passion." He pulled at the sheet, but she held fast.

"That would be a conflict of interest. I don't intend to spend my honeymoon waiting while you serve your time in prison."

"Where are you going?" He lunged, but she'd slid off the mattress, taking the sheet with her.

She wrapped it around her, toga-style. "To finish my bath."

"I'll have to find a good job so you won't be forced to wear rags like that."

Smiling, she let the sheet crumple around her feet, watching his eyes darken as he looked at her breasts, her legs. "I'm not worried about changing my lifestyle," she told him.

He dragged his gaze to her face. "Then what's the problem? Give me two good reasons we can't be married on your birthday."

She could think of only one. "You haven't asked me yet."

He sprang from the bed, catching her in his arms. "Miss Cecilia Hargrave Mason, may I have the honor of your hand in marriage?"

"Yes."

"Yes?" He repeated her answer as if he couldn't believe it.

"Yes, sir. Yes, please." She clasped her arms around his neck. "Yes, Mark."

"Is this an until-death-do-us-part or an until-my-boat-sails-again marriage?"

She answered him with a quick kiss. "My cousin Darryl is a minister; I'm sure he'll be glad to officiate. I'll call Grandmother and tell her we're coming to dinner, and we can announce the news to my family after dessert."

"Speaking of dessert . . ." His mouth feathered hers.

"You're only giving me three days"—she stopped, letting him nip her bottom lip before she continued—"to plan . . ."

His fingers caught her jaw, tugging her mouth open so his tongue could tease hers.

"We don't have time," she murmured unconvincingly when he walked her backward to the bed. "I need to wash my hair, finish my bath."

"A shower," he said, his voice as unsteady as his hands exploring her breasts. "Aboard the sub we take three-minute showers. Soap, rinse, dry. I'll show you how. Then again, I foresee certain complications, since it might take an inordinate amount of time to lather all these curves."

"We'll have the rest of our lives for this." She closed her eyes when his fingers brushed over her stomach and wandered lower. She stilled his hand with her own. "We have less than an hour; dinner is always served at the stroke of six in the Hargrave manor."

"We could skip dinner altogether."

"Sounds tempting but not practical." With one last kiss, she slipped from his arms and drew the sheet around her, tucking it under her arms as she stood. "Weddings don't plan themselves; we have things to do."

He grabbed the corner of the sheet so she couldn't walk away. "Why don't we do them first and tell your family later?"

He didn't relish the thought of suffering through a cross-examination in the Hargrave dining room. There were several things he needed to explain to Celie, among them the lettergram and her grandmother's absurd accusations about his financial affairs. Trying to discuss them in the presence of her grandmother could only court trouble. "I don't imagine your grandma will be as thrilled about the wedding as we are," he added, since Celie seemed seriously to consider his suggestion to wait.

Seeing her square her shoulders, he knew her answer before she spoke. "There's not going to be a *better* time. Grandmother will make a fuss if we tell her today; she'll do the same tomorrow." Celie once again let the sheet tumble around her ankles, smiling at him over her shoulder. "Don't worry. She's going to like gaining a grandson-in-law, although it might take her a little time to warm up to the idea."

Watching her walk toward the doorway, he stifled an urge to sweep her into his arms and demand they elope. If he did that, her grandma might think he was trying to outmaneuver her. This way, at least his cards would be on the table.

He wished he had one more day. Home in Arizona his brothers were collecting documents to fax, and by tomorrow he'd have the paperwork to prove to Grandmother Hargrave that his intentions were honorable, that what he needed was Celie, not Celie's money. If that didn't drive away the woman's suspicions, he'd just have to wait until the day he could place her first great-grandchild in her arms and hope her heart would soften enough then to realize he intended to stay at Celie's side, until death did them part.

Seated across the table from Mark, Celie fingered the stem of her wine goblet while she watched him. Determined to make the best possible impression on her grandmother, he'd insisted on wearing his dress blues. Devastatingly handsome, she thought, unable to keep from smiling.

Her mother and aunt were treating Mark with the respect they always displayed for dinner guests. Grandmother Grace ignored him altogether.

"Is wilted spinach still your favorite, dear?" Aunt Louise smiled as she watched Celie sample the salad. "I asked the cook to make it special, after you called."

"Frankly, we were quite startled to hear you'd be joining us for a weekday dinner." From her end of the table, Grandmother finally spoke. "May we also expect you for midnight services tomorrow?"

"Now, Grace, she may have other plans," Aunt Louise interceded.

"I need to give the cook a head count," Grandmother snapped. "If she's bringing guests this year, I need to know."

Celie refrained from pointing out the midnight Christmas buffet could easily feed three times the number of attenders. It didn't matter. Nothing mattered, except that she and Mark were getting married.

"I'm bringing my fiancé." She blurted out the words before she could stop them. Around her, the room stilled. Without looking, she knew Louise groped for the vial of smelling salts she kept pinned to her collar.

The maid recovered first, hastily exiting the room.

Fueled by Mark's encouraging smile, Celie met her mother's startled gaze. "We're getting married on my birthday. We considered eloping, but I wanted all of you to be present."

Katherine looked at Mark. "I assume you're the man in question, Commander?"

"Yes, ma'am. We'd planned to announce it after dinner. I'm sorry if it came as a shock."

"Hardly a shock." Grandmother glared at her sister. "If you're really going to faint, Louise, go do it in your bedroom.

Louise sniffed the uncorked bottle she held. "I'm fine. And I think this is simply wonderful. In fact, I'm going to be the first to welcome Commander Edwards into our family." After pushing back her chair, she stood and walked around the table, hugging Mark and then Celie. "Now tell me what I can do."

Celie patted her arm. "We want to hold the ceremony in the Florida room. I've already called Darryl and asked him to officiate."

"Nonsense. The Reverend Fallingsworth has presided over our family's weddings for the past thirty years." With a sharp look at Mark, Grandmother rang the crystal serving bell. "However, this isn't something to chat about over dinner. We'll discuss it later."

"Don't be ridiculous, Mother," Katherine admonished her before Celie could. "This calls for one of the bottles of wine Grandfather stocked for special occasions."

Grandmother shook her head. "If and when a wedding takes place, we will celebrate accordingly."

"We've already finalized our plans." Celie struggled to keep her voice patient, realizing she'd underestimated her grandmother's resistance.

"Nonsense," Grandmother said again. "It's impossible to schedule a wedding right now, Cecilia. We'll discuss this matter later. Eat your salad."

"There is nothing to discuss," Celie told her. "If you don't want us here, we'll go to City Hall. Mother, Aunt Louise, you're welcome to attend."

"On the contrary, our social calendar is already filled with obligations we can't ignore." With a warning glance at the maid entering the room, Grandmother lowered her voice. "We'll discuss this *later.*"

"There really is nothing to discuss." Celie shoved her chair from the table and rose. In seconds, Mark stood at her side.

"If you ladies will excuse us, we'll step out for some fresh air." Taking Celie by the elbow, he guided her out of the dining room and across the hall into the library.

"Your grandma seems determined to change your mind," he said, as he closed the door.

Celie sank into the closest chair. "She can't. I won't let her."

Standing behind her, he massaged her shoulders, trying to banish the tension he felt there. "Once I sail, you'll be here to face her alone until the spring."

"We've tangled wills before. She's hated every man I brought to dinner."

"Maybe I can sympathize with her, after all," Mark said with a wry laugh. "I'm just worried I'll get slapped with a divorce decree via satellite."

When she leaned her head against the chair back and looked at him, the love shining in her eyes took his breath away. "Why would I end the best part of my life before it begins?" she said softly. "Nothing she could say would make me change my mind."

He kissed her before he pulled her to her feet. "Then we'd better hightail it out of here and get to the store before it closes."

"What store?"

"The jeweler's. I'm going to buy a diamond to make our engagement official." He saw her smile dim. "What's the matter?"

Slipping her arms around him, she laid her head against his chest. "Diamonds are my grandmother's passion. I've always thought them cold and hard. Besides, I have a safety deposit box full of them left over from ancestors I never knew."

"Hargrave ones," he reminded her, trying not to think how paltry his would look next to those. He lifted her hands and examined her fingers, grazing the knuckles with his lips. "Those you wear for show. Mine you'll wear for love."

"Give me something else, then. Something personal." Her fingers smoothed over his, and touched his Naval Academy ring. "This."

He frowned. "It's too big—"

"But it's yours. I can wear it on a chain around my neck."

"I wanted to get you something special."

"It is something special, and it's yours."

Tomorrow he'd find her something better, something she deserved. After he wrestled the ring from his finger and gave it to her, she weighed it in her palm. "Consider us formally engaged."

Closing her fingers around it, he sealed the ceremony with a kiss. He broke away when he heard a knock at the door.

"Celie?" Katherine called. "May I come in?"

"Grandmother's sent an envoy," Celie murmured to Mark. "If I start caving in, pinch me."

After opening the door, Katherine peered inside, fidgeting with her pearl necklace as she looked at Mark, then at Celie. "I don't want to interrupt."

"Come in, Mother." When she did, Celie drew a fortifying breath. "I know this is sudden—"

"Sudden is hardly the word for it." Katherine lifted her hand when Celie started to speak. "I just wanted to tell you I'll take care of ordering the flowers, and the cook has agreed to prepare a few trays of hors d' oeuvres. Don't worry about your grandmother. She'll be fine, once she gets accustomed to the idea."

Katherine turned to Mark. "You'll have to excuse my mother, Commander. She sets grand goals for our family, and we can never quite live up to them."

"I think you're doing quite well," Mark noted.

"I learned long ago to push instead of pull." Katherine extended her hand. "Welcome to the family, Commander."

"Mark," he corrected, kissing her cheek. "Glad to be aboard. I guess I owe you a thank you for producing such a wonderful daughter."

"My pleasure." Katherine's voice faltered a moment, and her eyes glistened with tears as she hugged Celie. "It's about time someone special walked into your life."

Relieved to find her mother on her side, Celie smiled. "Thank you."

"Thank you for not eloping," Katherine said. "I learned the hard way a wedding should be a family celebration. You have family, Mark?"

"Besides my parents, there's my Grandma Tasha, three brothers, three sisters-in-law, seven nieces and nephews."

Katherine raised her eyebrows. "They'll find it impossible to get airline tickets this close to Christmas. I'll make arrangements for the corporate jet to fly them to Boston, and they're welcome to use the west wing for the length of their stay. Have your mother call me tonight and we'll iron out the details."

"Thank you, ma'am. She was heartbroken to think she'd miss the wedding." He felt like a boy finding a long-awaited puppy on Christmas morning and hoped Katherine's courtesy would be contagious and infect her mother.

"Let me know if you need anything else. Celie, your cousins wouldn't miss this for the world. Louise is already phoning everyone. What time is the ceremony?"

"Two o'clock," Celie told her. "Mother, we were planning on a small ceremony."

"It will be," Katherine assured her. "Just family. Now, have you thought about the cake?"

"No, we haven't."

"I'll order one right away. There's a chef at the Ritz who does wonders with live flowers."

Mark watched Katherine leave the room, then wrapped his arm around Celie's waist. "Let's go, honey. Looks like we've got us a *big* wedding to plan."

Celie stood before the bedroom mirror while Mark fastened the gold chain around her neck. The ring it held found a home in the shadowy cleft between her breasts.

"You deserve better," he said, nipping the nape of her neck.

"It will remind me of you."

"*I* want to remind you of me." Watching her in the mirror, he massaged her shoulders until she swayed against him. Unable to resist, he let his hands drift down toward her breasts.

She closed her eyes and rested her head against his chest. With one efficient motion, he unclasped her bra, then replaced it with his hands. Smoother than satin, he thought, his fingers drawing circles over her blue-veined skin. He brushed his fingertips over her nipples, and her sharp intake of breath matched his own. "I'm going to miss you, Celie."

"It's just three months," she whispered, trying to convince herself more than him. "Ninety days."

"Two thousand one hundred and sixty hours." More time alone than he wanted to think about. With his mouth, he skimmed the sensitive undersides of her breasts before he sampled the hollow of her throat where her pulse pounded.

Trailing his fingers over her stomach, he felt the muscles underneath flutter in anticipation when his hand rested on the elastic band of her panties. He tightened his hold to press her hips closer to him, her uneven breaths fueling his own desire.

"We'll have tonight and tomorrow . . ." For a moment she stopped breathing, watching in the mirror as he slipped one hand under her waistband.

He touched her. When she moaned, arching against his hand, he moved against her in return.

"After that, just memories." He let his fingers tangle and tease while his tongue traced the flush spreading over her neck. "Give me some to take with me."

She tried to match him touch for touch, but he wouldn't let her, wanting to give all he could before he took anything for himself. With his hands and his mouth, he incited her to the edge of reason until she twisted around, tangling her fingers in his hair to pull his face to hers. She kissed him, her body trembling against his.

Her hands clutched at his shoulders, her mouth searching for him as he carried her to the bed. Once there, she tried to kiss away the tiny red half-moons she had inflicted on his shoulders.

"Battle scars," he rasped, pushing her down onto the mattress. She arched her back when his mouth left hers to explore her secrets, to memorize what made her whimper, what made her writhe, what made her tremble and at the same time arch for more.

His hands became unsteady as they stroked her breasts, her stomach, the soft skin of her inner thighs. He couldn't begin to touch her enough, he knew, and then he couldn't think at all because she took him in her hands and stroked him until the tension in his muscles matched her own.

A sheen covered his body as he slipped into the silken warmth she so willingly offered. Locking his fingers with hers, he watched emotion play over her face as he gloried in the shudders racking his body, racking hers.

Whispering her name, he held her, burying his face in the hollow of her neck when her body went rigid, shattering her reason and his.

Afterward, he couldn't let her go, keeping her cradled in his arms as he shifted his weight and rolled sideways. Tired as he was, he kissed her thoroughly while he tucked the sheets around them.

"The blanket," she murmured wearily as she cuddled against him. "I think it fell on the floor."

Smiling, he rested his chin on her head and closed his eyes. "If you get cold, wake me."

Still caught in the vague world between slumber and wake, Celie touched Mark's shoulder, letting the solid warmth reassure her she hadn't dreamed yesterday. Then she yanked on the edge of the sheet in hopes of claiming a few more inches besides the too few she already had.

He stirred and kissed the curve of her neck. "It isn't even dawn," he whispered, his breath tickling her skin. "You're going to wear me out."

Almost four o'clock, she saw, looking over his shoulder at the dull red numbers of the digital alarm clock. "I shouldn't waste time sleeping."

"You've got it backward. Bachelors get premarital jitters. You're supposed to be planning your trousseau or something."

"There's not enough time to think about my trousseau or something."

Sighing, Mark lifted his hand and switched on the bedside lamp. "After I leave, you'll have three months to worry about all those little things."

"Most of those little things we should be planning together," she pointed out. "We haven't really talked about anything yet. Where are we going to live?"

He rolled over and buried his face in the pillow. "With each other."

She tickled his ribs until he turned again to face her. "I'm serious."

"So am I," he said sleepily. "I've been toying with the idea of going back to Arizona. There's an experimental energy program the Navy has its hooks in—windmill farms, solar cells, things like that—so I could finally put my engineering degree to use. I'd be mighty happy if you'd come with me." He smothered a yawn. "But I'm adaptable. If you want to stay here, we'll live in Boston."

Her mind whirled with other worries. "We should have eloped. Your family's flying in this afternoon, and Aunt Louise has called every one of my cousins. This is going to be the biggest small wedding Boston has ever seen."

"You can't have that many cousins."

Celie scooted up against the headboard and wrapped her arms around her knees. "More than you probably imagine. Let's see, on the Hargrave side, eighteen second cousins, twenty-two second cousins once removed, seventeen twice removed—"

"Twice removed from what?"

He sounded so bewildered she gave up. "Forget it. Someday I'll show you our family genealogy chart. Anyhow, I have nearly one hundred cousins I know of, although several no longer live in Boston."

Mark closed his eyes. "So they won't all attend the wedding?"

She decided not to mention, most, if not all, came home for Christmas. "You'll probably meet a few dozen at the wedding," she said, underestimating the number for his sake. "Maybe I'll ask them to wear name tags to make it easier for you to see who's who."

"You can't possibly know all their names."

Celie drew a deep breath. "Great-aunt Lydia has three children: Lydia Marie, Beatrice, and Frederick. I'll skip their spouses for now. Lydia's grandchildren are Karen, Will, and Fred Junior. Will's a lawyer, he graduated Harvard a year before I did. He has twins, Amy and Abby. Frederick married—"

Mark tossed his pillow at her. "I'm too tired to learn anything by rote. Get down here so I can go back to sleep."

When she slid under the sheet beside him, he kissed her, then switched off the lamp. "Besides, you lost me back with your Aunt Lydia. Why don't you write everything down and I can memorize it on the sub."

In the dark, Mark sought and found her mouth. He'd kissed her breathless before a thought struck him. "Just tell me there's no one in your family more domineering than your grandma."

"She rules the roost, although she's getting mellow in her old age, I think. She didn't fuss nearly enough about the wedding."

"Count your blessings." In the middle of the next kiss, he thought of another question. "Speaking of genealogy, how many children do we want?"

Celie considered, her hands sliding along the slope of his shoulders. "More than one. I hated being an only child."

"Two? Three? Seven?"

She clapped her hand over his mouth. "Let's start with one and work from there."

"Great idea." No longer sounding tired, he shifted her closer to him. "Are we trying first for a boy or girl?"

"I certainly didn't mean we had to start right now." She pushed halfheartedly at his shoulders. "We have too many other things to do today."

"First things first."

She felt her willpower dissolving as he caught her wrists and kissed her fingers. "Weddings don't just happen," she said weakly. "You have to plan them . . ."

"Your mother's taking care of everything." Mark tugged at the nightgown she had slipped on earlier after he'd drifted asleep. "What's this?"

"This, cowboy, is what Northerners wear to keep from freezing through long winter nights." He interrupted her laughter with a kiss that sent her senses cartwheeling.

Unhindered by the dark, his fingers coasted over the buttons. "That's my job, ma'am, keeping you warm in bed."

"I find that difficult to believe, since you hog the blankets when you sleep. I'll buy you a pair of pajamas to match."

When he pushed the gown from her shoulders, cool air rushed against her skin, making her breasts tingle. She arched her back when he took one in his mouth, the contact both searing and arousing.

He lifted his head, for a moment thwarting her efforts to kiss him. "Make sure they match the blanket, then, because they'll stay at the bottom of the bed. I've slept this way since I was a child."

"This way?" Her hands explored his shoulders, his chest, his hips. When she found him hard and ready she tried to sound surprised. "I thought you were tired."

"I can catch up on sleep aboard the sub. I'll miss you, Celie."

"I'll be here." His mouth was only a breath away from hers.

She lifted her head to close the distance and made her kiss an unspoken pledge. Grateful the dark hid the tears crowding into her eyes, she moved her fingers over his face, trying to memorize the feel of it. She needed something to remember, something to carry her through the long days and lonely nights ahead.

"I love you," she whispered, finding it really didn't matter that he tasted her tears when he kissed her again.

She wanted to linger this time, but her control slopped away, and she was helpless to do anything but follow his pace, hurled into pleasure so intense she she'd dissolved into infinite pieces.

Afterward, wrapped in his arms, she couldn't even move to sort the tangle of limbs and sheets. Against her breast she could feel his heart pumping like her own, each beat marking time before they'd part. "I wish you didn't have to go," she whispered to Mark.

"Time will fly."

She knew he was lying. Three months would seem a lifetime.

He pulled her even closer, tucking her body against his, smoothing a quilt over them both. "The Navy teaches recruits about sublimation, transferring instinctual drives into socially acceptable manifestations."

She bit his shoulder. "Speak English."

"Keep busy, you'll keep out of trouble."

"What kind of trouble?"

He slid his hand under the quilt until he found hers. "I have this recurrent nightmare you'll start analyzing everything and decide you've made a mistake, even before I get a chance to prove what an outstanding husband I'll be."

"Why would I do that?" she whispered, rubbing her chin against his knuckles. "It took me thirty years to find you."

"Suppose the magic wears off and you see all my faults."

"I'm looking forward to discovering each and every one." There was so much she didn't know about him, she realized. "What were you like as a boy?"

She felt him thread his fingers through her hair and fan it over her shoulders, across the pillow. "Typical all-American child, the boy-next-door type. Letters in track and football in high school, Eagle Scout."

Mourning all the years she had missed, she kissed his neck. Would she ever, she wondered, grow accustomed to the taste, the feel of him?

"I'm trying to impress you with tales of my youth, but if you keep this up, I'm going to have to impress you in other ways."

She laughed low in her throat. "What other ways?"

"I'll show you later." He hugged her, then walked his fingers over her spine. "I could keep you here for days."

"We have only two." The words sobered her. "And we might as well get up. It's almost six o'clock."

"You've just discovered my first fault," he told her. "On vacation, I sleep until the sun rises, and since we made love one way or another through most of the night, I'm not crawling out of bed until noon. A man needs his beauty sleep."

He sounded so drowsy she couldn't protest. She listened to his breathing until she knew he'd fallen asleep. Maybe, with so much to do the next few days, she wouldn't have time to think about his leaving. And maybe her grandmother would dance at her wedding.

Careful not to wake him, she climbed from the bed and pulled on her gown. His ring bouncing between her breasts felt intimately warm as she headed downstairs.

In the living room, she plugged in the tree lights and watched them twinkle. A tree without presents just wasn't a Christmas tree, she decided. She'd slip out today and find him a perfect gift, one small enough he could take on the sub, something special enough he'd remember her across the miles every time he saw it. Funny, less than a week ago she'd been counting the days until he left, but from a different perspective.

For breakfast, she settled on toast and tea. Later, when Mark awoke, they'd eat a real breakfast—more likely, brunch—at Vera's after they delivered her a handwritten wedding invitation. And she should call Shannon and share the news. After all, if her roommate hadn't let Mark into the house . . .

Refusing to dwell on what might have been, or worse, what might not have been, Celie carried her tea into the living room and switched on the CD player. Sitting on the sofa, she composed a mental list of things that had to be done. Find a wedding dress. Choose the music. Select the readings for the ceremony.

Lover, Wife, Mother. The words swam in her head, making other thoughts impossible. Christmas music swirled around her, creating a lovely background for the images flooding her mind.

A home in Arizona would be nice. Anywhere with Mark would be nice, although she couldn't begin to imagine what a windmill farm looked like. In the winter, maybe they could fly back to one of the quaint farmhouses scattered around New England and bundle their children in brightly colored snowsuits and boots for romps through snow-drifted fields. Summers they could visit Cape Cod to let their children frolic in the waves.

Still smiling a half hour later over her unborn children's antics, Celie jumped when the doorbell rang. She scrambled to answer it before the chimes woke Mark, but when she opened the door, Grandmother Grace's annoyed expression indicated she hadn't moved quickly enough.

Eleven

Well aware Grandmother never visited, only summoned, Celie tamped down a flutter of panic. "What a surprise—come in."

Wrapped in her ankle-length sable coat and tailed by her chauffeur, Grandmother marched inside. She swept a withered glare over Celie's rumpled nightgown. "I attempted to call last night, but I refuse to speak with a machine."

The phone had rung repeatedly, but Celie hadn't answered it, assuming various cousins were calling to offer congratulations. While murmuring an apology, she helped the older woman remove her coat.

"Wait outside," Grandmother ordered the chauffeur. "Keep the car running; I'll only be a moment." After he left, she looked around the living room. "Where's that young man?"

"Mark's upstairs sleeping," Celie said evenly, refusing to say more when her grandmother arched her eyebrows in tacit disapproval. "Would you like a cup of tea?"

"I'll be finished before the water boils." Grandmother sat stiffly on the edge of the sofa and rested her hands on the carved head of her cane. "Cecilia, I'm here to put an end to this nonsense about a wedding."

Knowing she'd feel better having someone on her side, Celie started toward the stairs. "I'll wake Mark."

"There's no need. This concerns your future, not his. Sit down, child."

It was a tone she knew better than to disobey. Celie sat.

"There will be no wedding." The older woman fluttered her hand to silence Celie's protest. "Believe me, I'm not saying this out of spite; I only want to keep you from making the biggest mistake of your life. That man is much older than you."

Celie's spirits were boosted by such a petty observation. If that was her grandmother's only objection, she could easily dismiss it. "He's nearly forty, but he acts my age. Wasn't Grandfather thirteen years older than you?"

"Those were different times. Besides, I'm not here to discuss my life, I'm here to salvage yours. That man does not have your best interests at heart."

Knowing anger would serve no purpose, Celie tried to keep hers from filtering through her words. *"That man's* name is Mark. He's warm and loving. I'm sorry you can't see him the way I do."

In the moments of silence that ensued, she fought to subdue her temper. Push instead of pull, she remembered her mother saying, and so she searched for the right words to describe Mark's outstanding qualities.

Grandmother spoke first. "Tell me how you met."

It would be so easy to fib and say she'd been introduced to Mark at the Christmas Ball, Celie knew. *What a tangled web we weave.* The words pricked her conscience into action. Leaving out the more intimate details, she explained how, aboard the cruise, she and Mark had met under a Caribbean sunrise.

"Did it not occur to you he might be—what is that word you children use these days—a gigolo?"

The outdated expression almost made Celie laugh. "A kept man? He's an officer in the United States Navy."

"Perhaps I've picked the wrong term. I meant a fortune hunter."

So that was it. Relaxing with relief, Celie smiled. "He didn't know me from Eve when we first met. Since I introduced myself as Celie Mason, he couldn't possibly have known I was a Hargrave."

"I see. Odd you failed to mention him to me or your mother after you came home."

Suddenly wary, Celie shrugged away the observation. "I've dated dozens of men without discussing them with you."

"I think it's safe to say you mentioned the ones you intended to marry. In fact, you usually brought them by for my inspection."

"I did not!" Although she felt like a reprimanded child, Celie gritted her teeth. The fact Grandmother had greeted her past fiancés with not-so-silent disapproval had nothing to do with Mark. Rather than argue that point, she tried to explain why she hadn't mentioned Mark earlier. "After the cruise, when we parted, I didn't expect to see him again."

"So he came to Boston uninvited?"

Concerned with what the woman *wasn't* saying, Celie worded her answer carefully. "His sub docked unexpectedly in Florida for emergency repairs and he flew to Boston."

She could tell the explanation didn't ease her grandmother's suspicions one bit but also realized it didn't matter. She wasn't marrying her grandmother, she was marrying Mark. "He was in love with me, and he knew, even before I realized it myself, that I loved him, too. I know it sounds too good to be true—"

"It sounds ridiculous. You're a grown woman in the eyes of the state, Cecilia, I realize that. I'm not asking for much, only that you wait six months before you marry. If this is really love, it will last that long, and I'll dance at your wedding. If it isn't, no harm done."

She wanted her grandmother to listen, to understand, to approve, but she wanted Mark more. "I've spent thirty years of my life without Mark. I know this won't be the big wedding you always hoped I'd have, but it's what I want. And I'm not going to wait. In a few days he'll be gone, and I won't see him again until spring. I'm not usually impulsive, but this time I'm trusting my instincts."

"You're not pregnant, are you?"

Celie bit back her denial at the unexpected question. "That's none of your business."

"So you aren't." Her grandmother ignored the rebuke. "Good, that's one less thing to worry about. Now, what have you given him so far?"

"Given him? My word."

"That's not what I mean." Grandmother thumped her cane against the rug. "Have you signed over stock? Offered collateral? Lent him cash?"

Her grandmother hadn't heard a thing she'd said about being in love. "From now on, my personal life is off limits," Celie said resolutely.

"You may think me a meddling old woman, but as long as I'm alive, I'll fight to the finish to protect the people I love. There's an envelope in my coat pocket. Bring it here, and then I'll go."

When Celie tried to hand it to her, Grandmother shook her head. "I don't have my glasses. Read it for me. It concerns your young man. I avoided making a fuss last night at dinner because you looked so happy, but he's flaunted the rules, and he knows the consequences."

Celie stared at the envelope, wishing she dared to toss it unopened into the wastebasket. "Consequences?"

"I suppose he'd thought I'd change my mind if you announced your engagement. Certainly doesn't know me very well, does he? Open it, child."

Hating herself, Celie did. She withdrew the papers inside and unfolded them.

Grandmother leaned forward. "A foreclosure notice, you see, for his father's property. I've taken the liberty of checking into his family's financial background. His brothers own two-bit ranches, and the commander has only a modest retirement fund. You're being wooed to save the family farm."

Once again her grandmother had taken it upon herself to meddle. Celie bit back an angry comment. More important, she decided, was proving Mark's integrity. There had to be a reasonable explanation. She flipped through the papers to find one. Her mind seemed numb, unable to function as she stared at a photocopy of Mark's birth certificate, another of his current bank statement.

"Cecilia, what plans has he made after he leaves the service?"

Trying to suppress the sense of uneasiness washing over her, Celie looked up from the papers. "Plans?"

"Job-wise. You can't live comfortably on his income, although he would certainly be happy living off yours."

Celie tried to recall the details of their early-morning conversation. "He talked about an experimental energy project the Navy is conducting with windmill farms."

Grandmother sniffed. "He's talked about many things, I'm sure. So did that other fortune hunter you nearly married, the one who wanted to be a doctor."

"That was different."

"The difference was that he'd have had to wait a decade before writing checks on your account. Commander Edwards, on the other hand, will be able to access your money the day he's married, which coincidentally is the same day you turn thirty."

She hated the bitter taste in her mouth. "One has nothing to do with the other."

"How do you know he's not going to sail into the sunset and hire a sleazy divorce lawyer to get a share of your money? Even though he can't touch your trust fund, you have other assets that would make quite a satisfactory settlement."

Her hands unsteady, Celie folded the papers and returned them to the envelope. "I appreciate your interest, Grandmother."

"No, you don't. You despise me at the moment. I don't want to hurt you, child, but I don't want to see you hurt, either. You know what happened to your mother when I didn't step in."

When Celie didn't answer, the older woman sighed. "Just wait six months. If he's not after your money, he'll come back and prove me wrong."

"If I can't trust him today, I can't trust him six months from now." Celie hated the way her voice trembled. She offered back the envelope, but her grandmother refused to take it.

"Keep it. It's of no use to me now. Get my coat, please."

After doing so, Celie summoned the waiting chauffeur and watched him assist her grandmother down the steps. At the bottom, the older woman turned to face her. "Don't be a fool, Cecilia," she warned. "Follow your head, not your heart."

Back inside, Celie switched off the Christmas music, then jumped when the doorbell chimed again, its notes depressingly cheery. Maybe, she thought as she hurried to answer it, Grandmother had returned with evidence to the contrary, or an apology and an explanation.

Vera stood at the door. She offered Celie a foil-covered platter. "Ham and eggs," she said. "Figured you two lovebirds wouldn't feel like coming out this morning, since the commander's got only a few days left before he sails."

Although the smell of the food turned her stomach, Celie accepted the platter and forced a smile. "Thanks, Vera."

Vera hesitated, twisting her knitted scarf around her fingers. "Saw that fancy car pulling away a few moments ago. You look kinda peaked. Not bad news, I hope?"

"Just family business." Celie belatedly remembered her manners. "Won't you come in?"

"No, I left one of the girls in charge of the kitchen, gotta get back. You bring the commander in for lunch today—I'm cooking up a pot roast special for him."

"I'll tell him." In the living room, Celie set the platter on the coffee table, then sank onto the sofa and dumped the papers from the envelope. She studied the incriminating facts a second time, desperate for a logical excuse.

She found none.

Her heart heavy, she unfastened the chain from around her neck as she climbed the stairs. In her bedroom, she switched on the overhead light, then held the ring high above the bed and let it fall soundly against Mark's quilt-covered chest.

A sleepy half smile curved his lips as he opened his eyes. "Couldn't wait until noon?"

She clenched her fists to keep from hitting him. "Wouldn't it have been less trouble to ask me for a loan? Or a handout?"

Blinking at her caustic tone, he bolted upright and searched the folds of the sheet until he found the ring. He weighed it in his palm as he stared at her. "What's this?"

"Something I haven't yet earned." The succinct speech she'd rehearsed as she stamped up the stairs fled her mind, leaving behind only savage words that couldn't begin to express her fury. "When were you going to tell me?"

"Tell you what?"

"Don't play me for a fool." She'd meant the words to be cold, but her voice thickened with unshed tears.

"Celie—"

"You'll probably get quite a kick telling the guys on your sub all about this."

After climbing out of bed, he grabbed his shorts from the floor and stepped into them. "About what?"

"Our marriage of convenience. Marriage for money. I don't know what they call it these days. It's been a few years since anyone's tried it on me."

The pain of betrayal no longer numbed her. She hurt. She ached. She hated being grown up, which prevented her from lunging and clawing at his chest, making him suffer as much as she did, if that would even be possible. She didn't think so. "I saw the foreclosure papers for your father's property. Grandmother brought them over a few minutes ago."

He sucked in a deep breath. "She's a suspicious old fool, and you're certainly doing your best right now to imitate her."

He caught Celie's arm when she turned away and forced her to face him. "There are two sides to every issue, and you haven't heard mine."

She shook loose. "You can explain everything while you pack. Boston's teeming with wealthy widows; you still have a few days to find one before you sail."

She snatched his duffel from the chair in the corner and tossed it onto the bed. It bounced once against the mattress, then tumbled to the floor, scattering its contents over the rug.

"Celie, listen." Mark kicked the duffel out of his way. "Come here, dammit. Stop running away from me."

Backed against the bed, she couldn't trust herself to look at him, let alone listen. Desperate for something to do, she knelt and began gathering his spilled belongings.

In a few strides, he stood over her. "Forget about that. We need to talk."

"It's all been said. Get dressed." Tears scalded her eyes, blurring her vision. She refused to look up, refused to give him the satisfaction of knowing she cared enough to cry. Instead she scooped his things into a pile.

A sock.

An opened package of chewing gum.

A neatly folded lettergram.

For a sickening instant, she couldn't touch it. When she did, her fingers shook while she unfolded it, trembled more while she studied the words she'd so carefully composed a month earlier.

Mark tried to haul her to her feet. "What are you doing?"

She realized he couldn't see what she was ripping into shreds, since her hair fell over her hands. "Tearing up the lettergram you never received," she said, as she stood. She watched him while she let the fragments flutter to the floor and waited for his denial.

He offered none. "Celie," he said, raking his hand through his hair. "Celie . . ."

Brushing her hands as if they were soiled, she turned away so he wouldn't see how humiliated she felt. "Get dressed. I'll call a cab."

He reached the door before she did and grabbed her by the shoulders. "Let me explain."

Her body rigid, she pulled free of his grasp. "No, let *me* explain." She managed to keep her voice cool, not revealing the turbulent emotions tearing her insides apart. "Somehow you found out who I was aboard ship. Must have thrown you for a loop when you received the lettergram and realized I wasn't going to marry you after all. Good thing the sub needed repairs so you could rush to Boston and change my mind. That about sums things up, doesn't it?"

She ran into the hall and down the stairs, not listening to him talk as he followed. After grabbing her purse from the parson's table near the front door, she whipped out her checkbook. "How much do you need? Seventy thousand? An even hundred?"

His mouth twisted. "Stop it. You're—"

"I'm sparing you the embarrassment of begging." She didn't flinch when he strode across the room and tore the checkbook from her hands. "I owe you something for all you've given me these past few days," she pointed out.

"I don't want a check."

She hated herself for not handling him with stony silence. "Of course not. I could stop payment the moment you set foot out the door. Cash?"

He started to grab her by the shoulders, then stopped, flexing his fingers, obviously making an effort to control himself. "I want you to shut up and listen."

"I've heard enough. Actually, I've seen more than I've heard. A foreclosure note is worth a thousand words." She found herself babbling to keep from doing something she'd regret even more, like stabbing him with her silver letter opener. Or crying.

He caught her chin, giving her no choice but to look into his eyes while he spoke. "My father's ranch has nothing to do with this. With us. Your grandmother's connected two unrelated incidents—"

She stiffened. "One of those *incidents* being our wedding, I suppose? Let me go."

He didn't. "I'm only asking for five minutes to explain."

"I've already given you several days. You should have told me you received the lettergram the moment I walked in and found you here."

"I should have, but I knew you wouldn't listen."

"I should have thrown you out then and there. Better late than never, don't they say?" That she'd been gullible enough to believe his stories infuriated her. She felt a renewed wave of anger wash over her. "You weren't really planning to come back in the spring, were you?"

"Of course I'm coming back."

"No, you aren't." She wanted her words to be sharp-edged, leaving no trace of doubt, but they wavered miserably as the fury drained from her. "Let me go."

He soothed her cheek with his fingers before he did. "Celie, I'd do anything for you."

"Stop." She wanted to plant her hands over her ears to block out his words. "No more lies, no more stories. Just go."

"Not when you're like this."

"I'm fine." She'd be much better if there weren't tears burning her eyes, sobs clogging her throat. "I was just fine before I met you, and I'll be just fine after you leave. I've had plenty of practice, don't forget."

"Stop it." Anger and frustration darkened his face. "I can't begin to count the number of times you said you loved me last night."

She refused to think about last night. "Love is based on trust," she lashed out. "Relationships are based on trust, and I have this incredibly old-fashioned theory that marriages should be based on trust."

"Have I asked you for anything?"

She ignored the hurt coloring his voice, reminding herself what he felt was no longer her concern. "That's not the point."

"It certainly is. If I wanted to make a quick buck, I'd have accepted your grandmother's offer."

"What offer?"

Closing his eyes for a second, he muttered a curse.

"What offer?"

He looked at her, his, eyes dark with regret. "It doesn't really matter now.

"Everything matters now. What did she offer you?"

"A settlement if I left Boston without you."

"A settlement?" At the moment, Celie would give anything to wash away the confusion disorienting her train of thought. "What did you tell her?"

"I didn't tell her anything. I don't want your money, I want you. Draw up some legal agreement to keep your trust fund out of my hands if you're worried. In fact, I insist."

"A prenuptial agreement?" She tried not to laugh. Money wasn't the issue anymore; trust was. And while his story about the bribe sounded outrageous, it also sounded suspiciously like her grandmother's handiwork. Funny Grandmother hadn't mentioned it. Then again, neither had Mark. "When did you speak with Grandmother?"

"Yesterday. She'd invited me to lunch."

Morbid curiosity warred with her ire and won. "Why didn't you tell me yesterday?"

His expression was grim. "Her accusations were so overblown I didn't imagine for a moment you'd believe them."

"Or maybe you were afraid I would." She drew back when he reached for her. Only anger kept her from dissolving into a huddling pool of tears, and if he touched her, she wasn't sure what she'd do, only that she'd regret it later. "Go get dressed."

She didn't have the energy to fight anymore, so she walked to the sofa and sat down. Aware he hadn't gone upstairs but stood and watched her, she busied herself with the papers on the sofa, sorting through the evidence, arranging it into neat piles. One was a listing of phone calls, no doubt illegally obtained but very revealing. "You called your brothers after you met with her," she noted aloud without looking at him. "All three of them. Guess you couldn't wait to share the good news."

"Once I learned she was investigating my family, I wanted them to be careful what they said."

"You called them again the night I decided I'd marry you."

"*We* decided to marry each other," he corrected. "I couldn't wait to share the news."

"For richer, for poorer. Guess we could eliminate the latter half of that phrase." Hearing her voice rise hysterically, she bit her lip hard enough to draw blood. The subsequent pain she felt seemed minor, nothing compared to the anguish slicing through her heart. She looked up to once again order him out of her house, out of her life.

He started to step closer to her, stopping when she held up her hand. "Dammit, Celie, I don't want your money."

"At least Derrick had the guts to confess once my grandmother turned over the evidence. He agreed to a payment-free loan to cover the rest of his medical schooling and set up a private practice. If you wanted more, you could have negotiated with my grandmother instead of—"

She had to stop, to swallow the bitter bile burning her throat. The times she'd bid farewell to the others had been clean breaks unhindered by the emotions that were now tearing her heart into jagged pieces. She lifted her chin and straightened her shoulders. "I think this time I've finally learned my lesson. Guess I owe you something for being such a good teacher."

"Celie, I love you."

"So you said." She wouldn't even listen to the words. Nor could she stand to look at him a moment longer, sleek and muscled, so handsome and so heartless. "You can't go outside like that. I'll call you a cab while you dress and pack."

He crossed his arms over his chest. "I'm not leaving yet."

She couldn't summon enough strength to argue. "Then I will. I'll stay at Hargrave Manor until you're gone. Feel free to use the house until you have to report back to base."

He looked at her a long time, a vein in his forehead pulsing. "Don't bother," he finally said. "I'll catch the first plane back to Florida, even if I have to ride in the cargo hold. It's been great knowing you, Celie. Look me up if you ever come to your senses."

Five minutes after he left, the doorbell rang. He'd forgotten something, she told herself, steeling her expression before she opened the door.

Her grandmother walked inside. "Is he gone?" she asked, without offering a greeting.

The tears Celie had managed to hide now refused to stop. Dabbing her eyes with an embroidered hanky Grandmother pressed into her hand, she nodded.

"You're doing the right thing," the woman reminded her. "If your mother had listened to me, her life wouldn't have been ruined."

"If my mother had listened to you, I wouldn't be here," Celie pointed out.

"Don't be impertinent." Grandmother checked her watch. "Our jet will touch down in two hours. Best call the airport and leave word for the crew to fly the family back to Arizona."

Celie knew she had no business feeling guilty for uprooting a family she didn't even know, for dragging them across country at Christmas just to send them back home. It wasn't her fault the wedding fizzled.

It wasn't theirs, either.

Mark had vowed to take the first flight to Florida. Was that before or after his family arrived? she wondered, then pushed the thought from her mind.

It was no longer her concern.

Logan Airport was so saturated with people clutching and kissing each other that Celie wanted to scream. She seemed to witness every joyful reunion as she headed toward the corporate wing.

The Hargrave Learjet was in a holding pattern and would land momentarily, an attendant tending the private lounge assured her. Clutching the bag she carried, Celie waited, staring out the plateglass window at the leaden sky.

Twenty minutes passed before the jet taxied to a stop. Watching the passengers disembark into the breath-catching cold, she assumed her hostess-best smile and readied herself to greet them. Before she was ready, the room swarmed with rambunctious children and harried adults trying to calm them.

A woman pushing a wheelchair calmly threaded her way through the crowd. "Miss Mason?" she asked when she reached Celie.

Celie nodded, staring into eyes the same marble-blue color as Mark's.

"I'm Mabel Edwards, Mark's mother. This is my mother-in-law, Grandma Tasha." Although she offered Celie a smile, her gaze flew around the room. "Where's my son?"

Celie heard the alarm underlying the woman's question. "He's fine," she rushed to assure her as she turned toward a tanned, wiry man who tapped her shoulder.

He looked her over, his face creasing in an approving smile. "You Mark's girl?" he asked, pumping Celie's hand without waiting for an answer. "I'm Mike Edwards. Welcome to the family. Where's that lucky son of mine?"

Before Celie could say anything he'd turned toward the other men in the room. "Doug, Dale, Bob—meet your future sister-in-law."

The audience grew by three men, each lean and tall as Mark, each towing a wife and children. Celie kept her smile through the introductions and, when they were finally finished, drew a shaky breath. "We were going to leave you a message—"

She couldn't finish, couldn't halt the tears splashing onto her cheeks.

Mabel stepped in front of Celie, shielding her from inquisitive stares as she turned to face her family. "You all go out and buy those children some souvenirs. Shoo, now. Miss Mason and I need to talk. You too, Mike," she added firmly when her husband started to protest.

When the room quieted, Mark's mother and grandmother watched Celie and waited for her to talk.

After digging a tissue from her purse, Celie wiped her eyes. "My grandmother wanted to leave a message for the pilot to take you back home. I guess that probably would have been the best thing."

Mabel sighed. "Mark's changed his mind again."

"No, he didn't." Her black eyes glittering, Grandma Tasha glared at Celie. "She did. Tossed him out like yesterday's garbage."

"Mother," Mabel scolded, offering Celie an apologetic glance.

"I did." With the admission, Celie readied herself for a rebuke.

"You don't have to protect my feelings," Mabel told her. "That boy was born with cold feet, I've always said, although he swears up and down he just hasn't found the right girl. He's never come so close to the altar before, so we thought maybe this time—" She stopped and shook her head. "I'm sorry," she said softly.

Celie tried to overlook the warmth in the woman's eyes that made it difficult to dislike her. "I'm sorry you came all this way. I've reserved suites for you at the Ritz-Carlton Club tonight. Our jet will fly you home tomorrow."

Grandma Tasha sniffed her disapproval. "Where's Mark?"

"I imagine he's flown back to Florida by now," Celie said.

"My grandson has more sense than that." Tasha wheeled her chair to the door. "He's in the terminal somewhere, I can feel it."

"Mother—" Mabel started toward the door, then shrugged when the woman pushed it open and wheeled through. She turned back to Celie. "You'll have to excuse my mother-in-law. Once she gets an idea, nothing can stop her."

Clearing her throat, Celie handed over the bag she held. "I'm returning the gift you sent and the stocking Mark's grandmother stitched for him. I don't imagine she'd want mine back, since my name's on it, but I'd be happy to reimburse—"

"Nonsense." Mabel pulled the gift-wrapped box from the bag.

After unwrapping it, she handed Celie a glass snowball. "Mark collects these."

All Celie wanted to do was bolt the room, but she made an effort to look interested and shook the globe so the artificial snow inside fell over a tiny adobe house and cactus garden. "It's very nice."

"I bought this one when he was young because every winter he'd wish it would snow in the desert. Not that he believed it ever would, mind you, but Grandma Tasha had him convinced dreams really do come true, and he wanted proof."

"By now he's discovered they don't, I'm sure," Celie said, tracing a pattern on the smooth glass. She'd learned the same thing as well.

Mabel shook her head. "I thought this would make a perfect Christmas gift for you two, since he said he'd finally found the girl of his dreams."

"I'm sure he will eventually." Celie handed the globe back, anxious to forestall the questions she felt the woman hesitated to ask. "The hotel limos will be waiting outside the main entrance. I'll call for a porter to get your bags."

Mabel clasped Celie's hand a moment. "I truly am sorry."

"So am I," Celie said honestly, although not for the same reasons. "It was nice meeting you, Mrs. Edwards."

Outside the lounge, she leaned against the wall and closed her eyes. Amid the bustle around her, she thought she heard her name called. Believing it was just her imagination, she opened her eyes anyway, then quelled a cowardly impulse to lose herself in the crowd. Instead, she lifted her chin and watched Mark weave his way toward her.

Twelve

"Hello, Mark," Celie said when he was within earshot. Her voice remained steady although her heart lurched at the hopeful look lighting his face. "The jet landed early, so I greeted your family. They're staying at the Ritz."

He reached for her. "Celie—"

She stepped away. "I just spoke with your mother. She knows we've canceled the wedding."

"Did you tell her why?" He supplied an answer before Celie

could. "Of course you didn't. You probably tossed her some incredibly polite inane excuse and ran away."

"Why it was canceled is none of her business."

"But it's mine." He moved closer, nearly pressing her against the wall but not touching her. "I still demand five minutes to tell my side of the story. Let me get my family settled in the hotel, then I'll meet you somewhere. Name the place."

If she dragged things out another minute, she knew her heart would shatter. Offering her hand for him to shake, she looked him square in the eye. "Mark, it's over. Good-bye."

"You're not going anywhere until we—" He stopped, interrupted by a nephew tackling his leg. The perfect moment, Celie knew, for her to drift away, except she found herself surrounded by his family.

"Already met your little lady," his father said, grabbing Mark's hand in a hearty shake. "Let's get some dinner and you can tell us all about her."

Separated by a wall of brothers, Mark's gaze met hers. She squared her shoulders, knowing she had nothing more to say.

Mrs. Edwards materialized at her side. "We need to visit the ladies' room first," she said. "You boys better fan out and find your grandma."

She walked with Celie to the closest restroom, then stopped outside. "I'm sure the last thing you feel like doing is joining us for dinner," she said. "Get going. Mark can make the excuses to everyone."

Nodding a grateful thanks, Celie turned and walked away. With tears clouding her vision, it seemed to take forever to wind her way toward the main entrance. When it was within sight, she nearly stumbled over the wheelchair that suddenly blocked her way.

Grandma Tasha cut short her apology. "So you think my grandson wants you for your money?"

Celie saw no sense in arguing or assigning blame. "I'm sure he's explained the situation to his satisfaction."

"Haven't found him yet," the older woman snapped.

"Then how did you know . . ." Celie let the question die since it didn't matter one way or the other. All she wanted to do was drag herself home and, put the entire week behind her. "If you'll excuse me."

"Not yet." The woman rolled her chair a fraction, just enough to block Celie's way again. "I'm an excellent judge of character, and I think you'll be good for him."

"He'll find someone else." The mere thought seared Celie's heart.

"Flying here, I read the tea leaves. You walk out of his life, he'll die a bachelor and you'll remain a spinster, crying yourself to sleep every night, dreaming about what might have been. Mind my words."

"I will," Celie said politely, deciding to humor the woman. The flight no doubt had pushed her into a sleep-deprived senility. "If you'll excuse me, I have things to do."

"No you don't." Tasha flashed a knowing smile. "You're just going to crawl home and curl up in your bed and spend the rest of the day crying. A shame to waste precious time when you both have so little. Why don't you and Mark make up today instead of tomorrow?"

The woman certainly had high hopes, Celie thought. This time when she excused herself, she veered around the wheelchair and headed toward the exit.

Her phone was ringing when she walked into her living room. Deciding not to answer it in case it was Mark, she listened to the recording instruct the caller to leave a message.

"Celie, Charlie Coffey. Tell Mark I've reviewed his application—"

She scrambled across the room to pick up the phone. "He's not here, Charlie."

"Hi, Celie. Merry Christmas. Just tell him there's no problem with approval of the grant, since his brothers' corporation agrees to contribute matching funds. I have a few documents he needs notarized—"

"He's not coming back."

A strained silence ensued, one she didn't even attempt to fill with explanations. No doubt the hastily planned, abruptly canceled wedding plans were already the talk of the city. Gossip would filter Charlie's way soon enough.

"He asked me to put a rush on this," Charlie finally said. "Did he leave a phone number?"

"He didn't leave anything." She'd told an outrageous lie, she realized. Everywhere she looked, Mark had left behind bits of himself. As soon as she replaced the receiver, she swept through the room, packing away the ornaments, tearing down the mistletoe.

She pulled her stocking from the mantel last, frowning at the bulge she felt in its toe. She reached into it and withdrew a folded note. She recognized Mark's handwriting, and although her common sense screamed for her to toss it unread into the wastebasket, she unfolded it and read what he'd written.

> *"I thought I could make you see we would be perfect together. My biggest mistake wasn't needing you, but thinking you needed me. What could I offer a woman who already has everything?"*

She sank to the floor, letting her tears blur the ink-written words. When she couldn't cry anymore, she rested her chin on her knees and looked around the room. She'd donate the tree to the city's mulch drive, and then her living room would be back to normal.

Enough already, she scolded herself. As she stood, she caught a glimpse of herself in the fireplace mirror and saw a stranger in the reflected image. Her hair tangled around her tear-stained face, her shoulders drooped, and her eyes were swollen and shadowed.

Time to move on with her life, she decided. Forgive and forget, that would be best. Forgiving would be easy. Forgetting, next to impossible. Every time she passed a Christmas tree . . . If she lived to be ninety, she figured, she'd only suffer through sixty more winter holidays.

She felt like crying again but found her self-pity wearing thin. If he just hadn't touched her so, hadn't taken a part of her soul with him. If he just would have accepted the money she'd offered, that would have wiped the slate clean.

"Sorry, Mark, your windmill farm's gone up in smoke," she said aloud, wishing fate had blessed her with the art of repartee. Then she could have said something he'd always remember and, as a finale, tossed the incriminating papers and the lettergram into the fireplace along with a lighted match. She could have shown him she could make a quick, painless break, as she had so many times before, starting with Charlie.

She stopped suddenly, staring at the phone as she replayed Charlie's message in her mind. Sinking to the floor, she gathered the papers she'd crumpled and started smoothing them flat, inspecting each one carefully.

Five minutes later, she grabbed her address book and leafed through it looking for Charlie's home number.

* * *

"You've a victim, Cecilia." Grandmother came straight to the point as she poured tea from the silver server. "There's no reason to feel guilty about sending him away."

"Guilty or not, I want to know what he said the day you lunched together. And what you said."

"I don't remember, dear. After all, I'm nearing ninety and my memory isn't quite what it used to be."

Although she knew her grandmother refused to forget anything, Celie ignored the outright lie. "Did you offer him money to leave Boston?"

"It arose, the fact his father needed cash to keep the bank from foreclosing on his family's property."

She'd never heard her grandmother skirt an issue before. "Did Mark ask you for the money, yes or no?"

"Outright, no. But there are more subtle ways to get what one wants."

She had no doubt her grandmother knew them all. "Did he say he'd consider your offer?"

"Not in so many words." Grandmother offered her a plate piled with delicate cookies.

Celie ignored it. "Exactly what did he say?"

"He said he wasn't hungry," Grandmother muttered.

Celie heard only what was left unsaid. "He walked out on you, didn't he?"

"I found him to be ill-mannered, disrespectful—"

"And not the least bit intimidated by you." For the first time that day, Celie found herself smiling. "Did he mention his brothers dabble in ranching as a hobby?"

"What difference does that make?"

"Apparently quite a bit, since you removed their corporate financial statement from the report you gave me. I stopped by the investigator's office and had him give me another copy."

She reached into her purse and produced a photocopied sheet. "Not only does their construction company have a satisfactory profit margin, Mark's brothers have agreed to underwrite a grant to match the government funding to experiment with alternative energy sources.

"Some of that money will go toward their father's ranch to pay off the mortgage. Mark didn't need a dime from you. Or me."

Not waiting for an explanation or an apology, Celie stood. "Maybe someday I can forgive you for meddling. Right now I have more important things to do."

***

The Edwards clan certainly hadn't been subdued by news of the canceled wedding plans, Celie thought. Standing outside the door to the hotel suite she could hear plenty of laughter inside. Steeling her courage, she breathed a quick prayer that she wasn't too late, then lifted her hand.

The door opened before she knocked. Grandma Tasha studied her a moment. "You're right on time," she finally said. "Told him you'd be meeting him downstairs for dinner."

"I wasn't—" Celie frowned first at the woman, then at the family crowding around the wheelchair. "I didn't tell anyone I was coming."

"Didn't have to," the older woman said smugly. "Go on, now. He's waiting for you in the restaurant, though I tried to get him to take you to that other place, the one with the violinist. How romantic can a place that calls itself 'The Dining Room' be?"

In the restaurant, the maître d' ushered her to Mark's table. As she approached, Mark stood and studied her with a wariness that made her throat tighten.

All she wanted was to throw her arms around his neck and beg him to come back into her life. First, she owed him an apology, so she let the maître d' seat her and allowed Mark to return to his seat. Watching him, she searched for something to say, the right words to express the sorrow locked inside, to seek forgiveness, to request another chance she didn't at all deserve.

"My grandma recommends the lobster au whiskey," Mark said politely, after several silent moments passed.

"I didn't come here for dinner." Celie drew a shaky breath and tried to decide where to start. "I found a report on your brothers' corporation."

"A bunch of overachievers." Mark sipped his brandy, watching her above the rim of the glass.

"Charlie called and said your grant will most likely come through."

"I didn't have any doubts."

She swallowed. "I guess you don't need my money after all."

His caustic glare said he never wanted it in the first place. If he'd just smile that smile, if he'd just offer a hint he might be willing to forgive her, she'd find it easier to say what needed to be said.

"I found your note when I—" She stopped, not wanting to mention her now-sterile living room. She pulled a note from her purse and offered it to him. When he didn't take it, she pushed it across the table. "I answered it. I was going to mail it to your base, but—"

But for some reason she couldn't explain even to herself, she'd decided to deliver it in person, even though her better judgment had insisted he had probably already hightailed it back to Florida. "I wasn't certain I'd find you here."

"My grandma talked me into waiting a day."

"She seems like a wise woman."

"Wise isn't the word." He took his time finishing the brandy, not once glancing at the note she'd put on the cocktail napkin in front of him. "Since you're here, you might as well deliver your message in person. One Dear John letter in a lifetime is enough."

She noticed his hand trembled as he returned the glass to the table and wondered if maybe he wasn't so untouched after all. The thought boosted her courage. "You asked what you could give me since I already had everything."

For a moment, it hurt too much to continue. He waited while she struggled to compose the next sentence. Belatedly, she realized she should have started by saying she was sorry, but she found her throat too tight to say anything without crying.

He finally spared her from doing either when he picked up the note. After unfolding it, he read aloud what she'd written. "A million tomorrows."

She didn't know what she'd expected him to do. Certainly not sit and stare at her answer as if she'd written it in some obscure language he couldn't comprehend.

She heard herself babbling to delay his devastating answer, if only for a few more minutes. "I'm sorry, I shouldn't have come. I should have mailed it, so you'd have time to think things over. Take your time, you can call or write when you get back to port, and if I don't hear from you, then I'll know—"

She couldn't continue. Clutching her napkin, she stood, her purse plopping from her lap to the floor, and when she bent to retrieve it, she found herself hauled to her feet. An instant later she was cradled safe and secure in Mark's arms.

"I don't need time, Celie," he whispered. "I need you."

In the middle of Boston's most elegant restaurant, she felt herself whirled around in the air, her hair tumbling loose from its French braid, falling over her shoulders as Mark kissed her. A long time passed before she heard the wine steward clearing his throat behind her.

Flushed and radiant, she returned to her seat, Mark to his. He looked at her, arching his eyebrows in a silent question when the steward presented a bottle of champagne. She shook her head.

"Compliments of the grandmother upstairs," he intoned.

"How did she know?" Celie asked Mark.

He shrugged. "Gypsy blood, remember?"

"More likely wishful thinking." She studied Mark's face, warmed herself in the smile that touched her heart. "I love you," she said, her words loud enough only to float across the table.

"I know." He took a gift-wrapped box from one of the empty chairs at the table and handed it to her. "You probably tossed all the Christmas things I bought into the trash, out of spite. Not that I didn't deserve—"

"I couldn't throw out anything. It's all packed in the attic. I was afraid I wouldn't have anything else to remember you by." Her fingers trembled as she unwrapped the gift and opened the box. Lifting out a glass snowball, she stared at the miniature brownstone inside that looked exactly like hers. A sleigh was perched on the roof, its reindeer team poised to leap toward the tiny winter moon.

"There's a man back home who custom-carves the scenery. I faxed him a photograph of your house, and he promised to have this here by Christmas. Mom picked it up for me. I know it's not much."

He was nervous again, she realized with surprise, as he fiddled with the silverware. She wanted to tell him he had so much to give, that her life had been so empty without him she couldn't imagine settling for anything less. There'd be time for that later, she decided. "I love it," she told him, running her fingers over the smooth glass while she watched the smile return to his face. "I don't have a gift for you."

"Yes, you do," he said, holding up the note. "I'll have this laminated—no, bronzed." He eyed a waiter hovering discreetly in the background, then looked at Celie. "Are you hungry?"

When she shook her head, Mark stood and offered his hand. "I figure with my family here and all the wedding preparations and Christmas Eve goings-on at your house, we'll need to carve out some private time to ourselves."

Pinning Aunt Louise's antique cameo to her collar, Celie studied her reflection in the cheval mirror. Over Grandmother's vehement reminder that several antique satin dresses waited in storage, she had chosen to wear her mother's wedding gown.

At the slightest movement, the gauzy gown swirled around her legs like a breath of air. She fingered the knotted flowers embroidered around the neckline, admiring the hours of painstaking work compliments of the communal family who'd witnessed her parents' vows.

For the tenth time, Vera, who was to be an attendant, fussed with the crown of fresh flowers resting on Celie's head. "You know your grandma's having a kitten," she murmured. "No veil, a peasant-style dress; she says next you'll be dancing barefoot down the aisle."

"I gave in when she wanted the wedding held in the front hall instead of the Florida Room," Celie murmured. She had more important things to worry about today than displeasing her grandmother.

At the knock at the door, Vera stepped back and nodded with approval. "Pretty as a picture. Just in time, too—look who's here."

Expecting Mark, Celie whirled around and stared at the blond woman who burst into the room. "I have a score to settle with you," Celie said. She tried to scowl at her roommate but ended up giving her a hug. "I didn't think you'd make it."

"I gave the cabby twenty dollars extra to get me here before the wedding started, and Vera promised to hold things up until I arrived. Congratulations, best wishes, now get going—time's awastin'." She gave Celie a gentle shove toward the door. "Your mother's waiting outside."

Stepping out of her bedroom, Celie drew a deep breath to settle her galloping pulse. Below, she could hear the orchestra's brass section begin the "Albason" fanfare.

At her side, Vera peeked over the balustrade at the crowd gathered below in the front hall. "My cue, I guess," she said, handing Celie a bouquet of scarlet poinsettias laced with baby's breath. Clutching her own bouquet of red poinsettias and holly, she started down the stairs, followed by Shannon.

Nothing to be nervous about, Celie assured herself as she smoothed her dress and took her mother's arm.

"I wish your father were here." Katherine blinked back tears. "Mother will never forgive me for not insisting Uncle Frederick give you away."

"I didn't ask Uncle Frederick, I asked you." Celie kissed her mother's cheek. "Let's go."

Gliding down the steps, Celie smiled at her aunts and uncles and cousins, at Mark's family, at the grandmothers all crowded into the front hall. When she reached the bottom landing, she could look at no one but Mark as he stood waiting at the minister's side.

A million tomorrows would hardly be enough, she knew. She slipped her hand through his, unable to look away from him, from the promise in his eyes, even when the ceremony began.

"Friends, we are assembled here . . ."

Vows. Pledges. Celie answered the minister's questions, barely aware of the words, blissfully aware of their meaning.

"With this ring . . ." She heard the love in Mark's voice as she accepted the plain gold band he slipped onto her finger.

". . . pledge thee my troth." Reveling in their power and promise, she repeated the vows to him.

". . . kiss your bride."

Trying not to burst with happiness, she kissed him, one final pledge to seal all the promises she'd made.

"I love you," she echoed his whisper again and again in between greeting guests and celebrating at the reception that followed.

Later, when it came time to head to the airport, she found the front door blocked by a wheelchair. Grandma Tasha looked at her, then Mark. "Perfect match," she said proudly.

"Perfect," Mark agreed, wrapping his arm around Celie's waist.

After lifting her face for Mark's kiss, the woman then clasped Celie's hands between her gnarled ones. "It's going to be a girl."

Celie blinked. "Excuse me?"

"The baby. It will be a girl."

Mark grinned. "Grandma, she's not pregnant."

Still holding Celie's hand, Grandma Tasha closed her eyes. "Katie Louise Edwards, born next year on Christmas Eve. She'll be a handful, because she'll have my gift, just as Mark does."

"Parlor tricks," Celie murmured, ignoring Mark's wide smile and biting back one of her own. She tugged her hand free. "Grandma Tasha, we have to go. Mark's plane will leave soon."

"Remember what I told you," Celie heard the woman whisper as she bid Mark good-bye.

Outside, Celie tugged Mark's sleeve. "Remember what? What did she tell you?"

"Limo's waiting," Mark said instead of answering her question. Inside the car, he settled back, shaking his head at her repeated queries.

When the car moved from the curb, he pulled her onto his lap. "I asked the chauffeur to take the long way to the airport. Grandma Tasha says the runways are being de-iced, so we'll have an extra hour or so."

The darkened, soundproofed middle window was raised, shielding them in their own private world, one Celie found warm and intimate. But Grandma Tasha's words tugged at her mind. "Tell me what else she said," she insisted.

Leaning his head back against the soft leather seat, Mark sighed with exaggerated patience. "She says you like Asian pears."

Celie kissed him. "So she's been interrogating Aunt Louise. What else?"

"You sunburn easily."

"Lucky guess, since my skin couldn't be much paler." She closed her eyes while Mark sampled it, fast losing interest in his grandma's alleged second sight.

Mark pulled her into his lap. "You've always longed for firelight and satin sheets when making—"

"She didn't say that!" Opening her eyes, Celie tried to pull away.

He held her close. "She brought a set of scarlet ones for our wedding gift," he said, laughing when Celie squirmed. "Too bad we won't have time to use them until I get back."

She knew she'd never be able to look Grandma Tasha in the eye again.

"I told her I didn't want to know any more," Mark said.

"Thank you." Her voice as uneven as his, she felt her skin heat as he brushed her face with his fingers.

"The thrill of the chase, so to speak. I intend to uncover your fantasies myself, one by one. How many do you have?"

Her breath hitched when he nipped her earlobe. "A million."

"Nine hundred ninety-nine thousand nine hundred and ninety-nine," she corrected several breathless moments later. "I love you, Mark."

"If that's all it takes to make you say it . . ."

She caught his hands and pressed a kiss to each palm. She'd soon be waving goodbye to a jet carrying him back to Florida. All day she'd refused to think about the inevitable; now it was facing her as they drew closer to the airport.

"Don't think about it," he whispered, his lips a breath away from hers. "In three months, I'll be back."

Till death do us part. The vow he'd made earlier echoed soothingly through her heart as she snuggled against him. "I'll be waiting," she promised.